The Strange Malady of Alessandro's Uncle
and *Other Stories*

By the same author

Fiction

Axton Landing (Book One of Adirondack Trilogy)

The Railroad (Book Two of Adirondack Trilogy)

Forever Wild (Book Three of Adirondack Trilogy)

Blame A Novel

The Bethune Murals A Novel

Non-fiction

Proceed with Caution: Predicting Genetic Risks in the Recombinant DNA Era

Promoting Safe and Effective Genetic Testing in the United States (with Michael S. Watson)

Assessing Genetic Risks: Implications for Health and Social Policy (with Arno Motulsky, Jane Fullarton, Lori Andrews)

The Strange Malady of Alessandro's Uncle
and Other Stories

by

Tony Holtzman

CLOUD
SPLITTER
PRESS

Cloudsplitter Press, Menlo Park CA
www.cloudsplitterpress.com

For individual orders: www.thebookstoreplus.com or
www.amazon.com

Bookstores can order from www.northcountrybooks.com

For more information visit cloudsplitterpress@gmail.com

ISBN 978-0-9984893-6-0

Library of Congress Control Number: 2020906688

To

Eva Cohen, 1965-2019

designer par excellence

CONTENTS

Preface

In 2006, I was invited to speak at the Fourteenth World Congress on Psychiatric Genetics in Sardinia, Italy. Having retired from the active faculty at The Johns Hopkins School of Medicine in 2002, I was looking forward to travel while transitioning to a new career in creative writing. Barbara and I had never been to Sardinia and combining a touristic trip with the opportunity to express my concerns about "genohype"—the tendency of the media and many scientists to exaggerate the benefits of genetics to humans—was an offer I couldn't refuse. I accepted and submitted as a title, "Genetic Tests, Commercialization, Conflict of Interest, and the Role of the Media." I started to prepare a traditional scientific talk, but as I flexed my creative writing muscles I hit on a novel idea: tell a fictional story to make my point. What better place to set the story than in Sardinia? I did some research about the island, its population, and principal occupations, and concocted a not implausible plot.

If nothing else, my talk was a break from the tedium of standard presentations and was greeted with chuckles, some outright laughs, and generous applause. With a few changes, I wrote up the story and submitted it to BMJ (British Medical Journal), which publishes a satirical issue every December. The story appeared under the title, *The Strange Malady of Alessandro's Uncle*, the opening bookend of this collection.

Not all of these stories have points. Take the closing bookend, *The Nobel Prize in Literature*. Scientists and novelists dream of winning the Nobel Prize in their respective fields and I was no exception. For the vast majority of dreamers, including me, the prospect is ludicrous, which makes the dream ripe for satire or fantasy. My story attempts both. Although it portrays blatant ageism, it's ending is intended to leave the reader wondering whether Albert won the prize or not. Among the few readers I've polled, there is no consensus, which pleases me no end.

The stories between the bookends are a motley collection; eclectic might be a more refined adjective. Most, but not all are drawn from experience—my own and others I've known—tempered with imagination. Unlike writers who dismiss making points as propaganda, I don't think it a sin to expose my own beliefs as long as I can find a clever, engrossing way to engage readers without preaching. I've attempted this with *Brahms' Fourth Symphony,* and *A Foot in the Door* (sexism); *See Jane Run* (racism); and *Only a Game* (reality television), although these are not always the main themes.

I wanted to write a story in which climate change was a major factor. I started with a question— what would happen if an electrical grid serving the entire country collapsed because of heat waves? Transforming experience and research into imagination, the real pleasure of writing fiction, resulted in *A Cascading Failure*.

Sometimes I'll start a story without a point in mind. I began what is now *Last Days of Summer* over ten years ago as a story of suspense, originally titled, *Last Man on the Mountain.* The bitter 2016 Presidential election campaign provided a context in which I could question the rigidity of the assumptions we make about unfamiliar people. From the start, the story drew on my experience—summering in the Adirondack Mountains and aging. My first-hand experience with aging also figures in *The Boy Friend* and *The Umbrella,* as well as *The Nobel Prize in Literature.*

If the stories get you to think a little, even if they get you angry, that's great. But most of all, enjoy!

Tony Holtzman

Menlo Park CA

March 1, 2020

Postscript, May 20, 2020. These stories were completed before Covid-19 struck. The isolation that ensued as people sheltered in place was not unlike what I envisioned in *A Cascading Failure.* The failure of the electric grid and the pandemic both stemmed from what some call progress and others overreach—an insatiable demand for electricity in one case and globalization in the other. In both instances, American society ground to a halt. But there was one important difference. In my story, people had no choice; the means to social intercourse collapsed along with the grid. As Covid-19 progresses, people have become increasingly restive under isolation, fearing another Great Depression. After one year without electricity, the future of American society seemed doomed in my story. Let us hope that is not the case in the aftermath of Covid-19.

The Strange Malady of Alessandro's Uncle

Had Alessandro not filed his story, Professor Johnson's talk would have gone unnoticed. Despite its bold title, "A Gene for Schizophrenia," it was only one of several hundred papers and posters, some equally boastful, that were being presented in simultaneous sessions at the International Congress of Genetic Psychiatry in Cagliari, Italy. It was the location of such meetings rather than the presentations that attracted physicians and scientists often accompanied by their spouses, or sometimes their mistresses. Except for the speakers immediately before and after Johnson, most of those present at the start of the session had already left for more touristic attractions. Alessandro, recently graduated from college and now a reporter for L'Unione Sarda, the local newspaper, was one of the few who had stayed. And with good reason.

*

A month before the Congress, Alessandro, in leather jacket, khaki pants, and sandals, had driven his motorbike to visit his uncle, a goatherd in the mountainous Barbagia of Sardinia, arriving shortly before noon. He removed his helmet, his long black hair tumbling down, and walked along the rocky footpath to his uncle's hut. His uncle was sitting on a stool at the head of a rough-hewn plank, propped up on two crates. With unkempt gray hair and a wispy, goat-like beard protruding from his weather-beaten face, he wore a moth-eaten woolen shirt, ragged at cuff and collar. On each of the other three sides a goat stood, its forefeet firmly planted on the plank, its hind legs on the earthen floor.

A gust of wind through the open door blew a rectangular piece of paper toward one of the goats, who used a forefoot to gather it toward his mouth. "Should he be eating that?" Alessandro asked. His uncle pulled the paper from the goat's mouth before he could chew on it and handed it to Alessandro, who smoothed it out on the table. "It's a prescription dated more than a month ago with your name on it. Were you sick?"

The goatherd, a man of few words, a man who had never married and who stolidly followed the same routine day after day, replied, "No."

"Had you gone into the village to see a doctor?"

"No."

"Then where did you get the prescription?"

"Qui."

Alessandro was incredulous. "Here? In your hut?" His uncle nodded.

"Who gave it to you?"

"Un'infermiera."

"A nurse? Here in your hut?" The old man nodded.

Alessandro took the prescription back to his desk at L'Unione Sarda. He googled the name of the drug and the first of many listings flashed up on his computer screen. He clicked on one, then another. They all said the same thing, astonishing Alessandro.

He learned that the drug, Olanzapine, was an antipsychotic used to treat schizophrenia. "It works by decreasing unusually high levels of brain activity," one listing said. Alessandro was surprised that his uncle had a high level of brain activity. He made an appointment to see the doctor who had signed the prescription in his office in Cagliari, and they met two weeks before the Congress. The doctor peered at the prescription, stroked his beard, and then told Alessandro how he had come to diagnose schizophrenia in his uncle. Using his journalistic skills, Alessandro made other inquiries and pieced together the story of his uncle's diagnosis.

A few weeks before Alessandro's visit—after the winter snows had melted off the peaks of the Gennargentu—a public health nurse from Cagliari made her calls through the Barbagia. She knocked on the door of his uncle's hut, and he commanded, "Avanti." After her eyes became accustomed to the dim light, she saw three goats, each standing with its forelegs on a side of the table, sipping milk from their bowls. Sitting at the head, the goatherd seemed to be listening to the goats as they slurped their milk and made goat-like noises. He responded in a language the nurse did not understand; she wondered if it was gibberish.

Days later, she returned with the doctor. After introducing him, the nurse urged the goatherd to continue his lunch as she and the doctor retreated to the shadows in the one-room hut. They heard him talking to his companions. The doctor thought the goatherd was speaking logudorese, an ancient Sardinian dialect. There were long pauses in which only the goats' slurping could be heard. When the old man had finished his lunch, the doctor asked him a few questions, had him stick out his tongue, and then wrote the prescription, which he handed to the goatherd.

Alessandro had the prescription filled and a few days before the Congress returned to the Barbagia and instructed his uncle on taking the medicine.

*

When his paper was announced, Professor Johnson, rotund in his dark, three-piece business suit and tie, strode to the podium and adjusted his horn-rimmed glasses. Using PowerPoint® slides, he described how he and his colleagues had studied the genes from a large number of schizophrenic patients, as well as their normal parents and siblings. The schizophrenic patients were six times more likely to possess a genetic variant than their unaffected relatives. He went on to predict that within a year, a test to detect the presence of Schizo-12 (as they called the variant) would be on the market, and a drug that would prevent schizophrenia in patients who tested positive could be expected within five years. He concluded by thanking Psychotropics-'R-Us, an American pharmaceutical company, for supporting the work.

When the session ended, Alessandro introduced himself to Professor Johnson and in tolerable English asked if he thought a man who discussed matters with his goats was schizophrenic. Johnson thought for a moment. "Well, I'm not a psychiatrist, you know," he paused, gazing momentarily at the ceiling, "but keeping goats for pets

is unusual to begin with. I'd say he probably was."
(Only later, when he returned to his desk at L'Unione
Sarda, did Alessandro realize that he had neglected to
say that his uncle was a goatherd. Would that have
changed Johnson's diagnosis? he wondered.) "

"And you now have discovered a gene for
schizophrenia?"

"That's right," Johnson replied.

"Well, that man I just told you about, with the
goats, is my uncle on my father's side. Does that mean
that I could have the Schizo-12 gene, too?"

Johnson thought for a few seconds. "If your
uncle inherited it from your father's father or
mother—your grandparents—yes, you could. Is there
schizophrenia in your family?"

"Other than my uncle, not that I know of; my
uncle doesn't have kids. I'm the oldest in my
generation."

"How old are you?" Professor Johnson asked.

"Twenty-five."

"Tell me, do you ever see things?"

"Only what's there. Do you mean
hallucinations?"

"Yes, that's what I meant. Are you ever
depressed?"

"I worry I'll lose my job." Alessandro looked
at his watch. "Excuse me, Professor. If I don't file my
story soon, I might."

By the time he reached his desk, he was so sure
he had signs of schizophrenia that he was ready to
consult a psychiatrist. Still, he managed to put aside his
fear and write up Professor Johnson's lecture.

The story appeared under Alessandro's byline
in the next edition of the paper and on its website. It

was picked up almost instantly by Corriere della Sera, Italy's leading evening paper.

On his way to his girlfriend's apartment that night, Alessandro passed an old woman sitting on the stoop of her house feeding milk out of a bowl to two cats, telling them how good they had life. Does she have schizophrenia? he wondered. If she does, it's a very common disease.

*

Cavorting around Sardinia while Johnson spoke, most Congress participants were greatly surprised when they picked up the International Herald Tribune outside their hotel rooms the next morning and saw the headline on the front page: "GENE FOR SCHIZOPHRENIA FOUND." After reading the full story, a few Congress participants e-mailed their stockbrokers in the United States to buy shares in Psychotropics-'R-Us. It was three o'clock in the morning in New York.

A few hours later, the story was on National Public Radio's Morning Edition. ABC-TV had awakened a well-known American psychiatrist and arranged to bring him to the nearest studio, where his comments on the report were viewed by millions on Good Morning, America. Rubbing his eyes, the expert said he awaited details of the report, but if the results were confirmed, the findings were "very exciting."

Psychotropics-'R-Us stock opened on the New York Stock Exchange that morning at $4 a share. It closed at $26.

The president of the Congress and Professor Johnson were inundated with phone calls and e-mails. The president decided to convene a special public session the following day at which Professor Johnson would summarize the findings and the president would invite questions. Two of Johnson's co-authors, one from France and the other from the United Kingdom, flew to Cagliari, as did the scientific director of Psychotropics-'R-Us.

Held in the largest ballroom of the hotel that served as the official headquarters of the Congress, the special session was filled to overflowing. Reporters, Alessandro among them, sat on the floor immediately in front of the makeshift dais while photographers and television cameramen stood along the sides. All the seats were filled and some people stood in the back. Despite the air conditioning, the room soon became rank. The lights in the enormous crystal chandelier dimmed to signal the start of the session and the TV cameramen turned on their Klieg lights, aimed at the dais. The president of the Congress, speaking in Italian-accented English, introduced Professor Johnson and his collaborators. Wearing the same three-piece suit and tie from the previous day, Johnson summarized his group's findings and showed the same slides that had accompanied his paper, repeating the prediction that a test for Schizo-12 would soon be developed, followed by a drug for the prevention of schizophrenia.

"The floor is open for questions," the president announced when Johnson had finished. Several microphones had been mounted on the floor of the ballroom. The first few concerned the DNA analyses and other aspects of methodology. Johnson and his colleagues answered them with ease.

A reporter, in shirt sleeves, seated on the floor in front of the dais, raised his hand and was directed by the president to the nearest microphone, "You call this gene variant 'Schizo-12.' Are there eleven others?" he asked.

Johnson replied, "Yes and no. Let me explain. The variant we call Schizo-12 is a variant of a gene we call 'Schizo.' Other groups have found variants that seemed to be associated with schizophrenia, but the reports were not based on as large a number of patients. Some of the claims have since been retracted."

The reporter followed up. "What was the basis for the retractions?"

Johnson turned to his British colleague, who answered from the dais. "One reason was misclassification of patients. Controls who didn't have the predisposing variant were diagnosed with schizophrenia after the study was completed . Other patients who were classified as schizophrenic and had the predisposing variant were later reclassified as normal. Some of them had hallucinations due to drugs or environmental toxins, not schizophrenia."

Another reporter attracted attention without going to a microphone. "Professor Johnson, two questions," he shouted. "First, have you filed for a patent on the Schizo gene? Second, do you hold stock in Psychotropics-'R-Us?"

Johnson was starting to perspire. After initially hesitating, he replied, "Yes, to both questions. The patent is held jointly by me and my colleagues, and by our respective universities. Psychotropics-'R-Us has been given an exclusive license to the gene, including variant forms. As part of the agreement, my colleagues and I and our universities received shares of stock in Psychotropics-'R-Us."

The president seemed surprised. He turned to

Johnson, "How can you patent a gene? That's a discovery not an invention."

Johnson's French colleague, slim and dapper, came to the dais to reply. "That's a very good question. Patents on sequenced genes have been challenged in Canada and at the European Patent Office. But they are still being issued."

Dressed conservatively in a gray slack suit, a prim woman made her way to one of the floor microphones. "Dr. Johnson, doesn't the fact that you own stock in Psychotropics-'R-Us pose a conflict of interest?"

"Madam—" he started.

"It's Professor, at University College London," she interrupted.

Johnson took off his glasses and mopped his brow. "Professor, if you are insinuating that I or my colleagues fabricated results, I find that highly insulting."

She held fast to the microphone and responded before the president could call the next person. "No, I am not insinuating that you fabricated results, but your prediction that a genetic test might soon be on the market, and that a drug is anticipated for those who test positive, seems very self-serving if Psychotropics-'R-Us is going to market both the test and the drug." She walked away from the microphone.

Johnson hesitated, and the president, hoping to avert a confrontation, called on the next questioner, a graying Congress participant from the University of Bologna who wore a sports coat but no tie. "Your slides showed the frequency of the Schizo-12 variant in the general population to be ten percent," the professor stated, "and the occurrence of schizophrenia to be one percent, forty percent of whom had the variant. Under those circumstances, I have calculated the chance that any person who has the variant would develop schizophrenia to be only forty percent, or one in twenty-five."

Johnson's British colleague shot back. "But they have six times the risk of their relatives without Schizo-12."

Undeterred, the Bolognese professor replied calmly, "That may be, but if you are going to prescribe medication for healthy people on the basis of a positive Schizo-12 test, ninety-six of them would never get schizophrenia." He turned and walked away from the microphone. A murmur went through the audience. The president thanked Johnson, his colleagues, and the audience for their interest and adjourned the special session.

Alessandro buttonholed the Bolognese professor and asked him to explain his calculations. He led Alessandro to two adjacent chairs in the now empty ballroom, borrowed his notepad, and with his pencil drew a grid with four columns and four rows, filling in the cells with numbers derived from the percentages he had recited on the floor. He returned the notepad to Alessandro.

Changing the subject, Alessandro asked, "So tell me, Professor, do you think that a goatherd who talks to his goats while he feeds them has schizophrenia?" (This time he remembered to mention his uncle's occupation.)

The professor laughed. "About as much chance as a widow who talks to her pet cats while they sip the milk she has put out for them." Reassured that neither he nor his uncle had schizophrenia, Alessandro decided he did not need to consult a psychiatrist.

None of the news stories that appeared after the special session mentioned the Bolognese professor's calculations or his conclusions. Alessandro brought the notepad on which the professor had drawn his grid to a prominent statistician in Rome, who confirmed the calculations. A month after the Congress, Alessandro submitted a story questioning the "validity"—a term he had learned after talking with the statistician—of a test for Schizo-12 to a weekly news magazine. The story was never published. Only later did he discover that the magazine's publisher was a major shareholder in Psychotropics-'R-Us.

*

The company's stocks hovered around $25 a share for the next two years. The company then started to offer a test for Schizo-12 to the general public, and its stock quickly rose to $40 a share.

Several healthy people who were tested for Schizo-12 committed suicide shortly after learning their results were positive. The presence of the variant in some of their older, unaffected siblings suggested that they would not have developed schizophrenia. In other cases, families of people who developed schizophrenia brought suits against Psychotropics-'R-Us because their test results were normal.

Three years after the Sardinia meeting, Psychotropics-'R-Us sent the U.S. Food and Drug Administration data from clinical trials to demonstrate the safety of its new drug for counteracting the effects of the Schizo-12 variant. Concerned about the high percentage of healthy individuals falsely predicted by the test to develop schizophrenia, and about the sixty percent who were diagnosed with schizophrenia despite a negative test result, the FDA requested that the company withdraw the test and refused to let a clinical trial proceed until the company could improve the test's validity. Before long, the company's stock fell to $2 per share and Psychotropics-'R-Us abandoned its test for Schizo-12.

After the Congress in Sardinia, Professor Johnson and his collaborators recruited twice as many schizophrenic patients and controls as they had for the Cagliari paper. They submitted an abstract of the results to the next International Congress in Bangkok, four years after the one in Sardinia. In this new, larger group, the chance of schizophrenia was only 1.2 times higher in those with the Schizo-12 variant, compared to those without it—not statistically significant. The abstract was not accepted for presentation. Psychotropics-'R-Us filed for bankruptcy.

*

Although Alessandro had doubts that his uncle had schizophrenia, he thought that if he did, the drug should have cured him by the time the medicine had run out. One Sunday, as winter approached, with his girlfriend's arms wrapped around him, he returned to the Barbagia on his motorbike. They found his uncle, once again, in conversation with his pet goats, an empty medicine bottle visible in the background. After the customary hugs and greetings, Alessandro pointed to the bottle and asked, "Have you taken all the pills?"

"Certamente," his uncle replied gruffly.

"How do you feel?" Alessandro's girlfriend asked.

"Mi sento bene."

Alessandro decided there was no point in refilling the prescription.

The Boyfriend

For the first year after Lisa died suddenly of a stroke, Jeff could only think about whether his wife of fifty years had suffered. Did she have a severe headache? Did she become paralyzed? Did she realize she was about to die? His medical friends could not give him definitive answers. Only mid-way through the second year did the thought strike him that he might never again sleep with a woman he loved. He then had a succession of brief relationships with women his age, only to find that none of them had his wife's intellectual and emotional depth, or her physical beauty. Up until her death, Lisa had appeared to him in youthful guise, a visage he could not possibly see in women of his age whom he had known for only a short time.

Their children surprised the widower with an eightieth birthday party. His eldest granddaughter gave him a recent biography of Benjamin Franklin. The gift rekindled his interest in American revolutionary history, which he had taught before retiring, and he endeavored to learn more about one particular aspect of Franklin's life.

The public library in Jeff's suburban town was able to locate and obtain copies of documents relevant to his research. The library was not close enough for Jeff to walk there, but he was able to ride his bicycle to the leafy park that surrounded it. The park had a playground for toddlers, and a gaggle of geese. A spring-fed brook flowed through it.

Jeff would lock his bike to the rack in front of the library and walk into a spacious, contemplative, carpeted room divided into alcoves, each furnished with a long oak table and armchairs. Customarily, Jeff took a seat in an alcove facing the reference desk in the center of the room. Cathy W.—the name on the plaque she placed on the reference desk at the start of her shift—seemed genuinely pleased when she retrieved documents for his research project, cheerily bringing them to his table when they arrived a few days after his request.

Cathy was, he guessed, in her thirties. She had luxuriant, shoulder-length brown hair. When he approached her with a request, she greeted him with a radiant smile. She did not need or wear makeup. "What can I help you with?" she would ask in a contralto voice. If his query required a search of the reference shelves, she stood. Usually she wore knee-length dresses that did justice to her figure. One that Jeff particularly liked was dark brown with a column of large, round, white buttons down the front. He followed behind her, noting the gentle sway of her hair, the graceful swing of her hips, and her perfectly shaped legs as she searched for whatever book he had requested, invariably finding it and handing it to him, again with a smile.

"Thank you so much," he would reply, taking the book.

"Any time. Anything else I can help you with?" she would ask pleasantly, but not flirtatiously. He noticed she was not wearing a wedding band.

Jeff became infatuated with Cathy. Looking out on the world with a youthful mind— neglecting the fact that it was lodged in the body of an old man—he felt sure she was more cordial to him than to other library patrons. Buoyed by hope, Jeff became certain that Cathy had a lot in common with him; the same taste in food, music, and politics. One night, he dreamed he was walking with her through a sunlit meadow with lush mountains beyond. They picnicked under the shade of an old oak tree. Cathy recited poems to him. They made love on a pile of hay in an old deserted barn. When he tried to undo one of the large white buttons on her brown dress, she turned so he could unzip it from the back. As he emerged from sleep the next morning, he felt his hand caressing Cathy's smooth skin. When he opened his eyes, it was the pillow.

He wanted to advance his relationship with Cathy, but how? *Inviting her to lunch or coffee seems innocent enough. If she refuses, that will end it and I'll stop imagining. If she agrees, what would we talk about? What if she seems amenable to starting an affair?*

No, she'd say the idea was absurd, pointing out that I am probably older than her father, that she is happily married with two kids, or maybe she's a lesbian. She might get up and leave before we are even served.

He became so dismayed that he had trouble focusing on his research project and stopped going to the library. Banishing thoughts of Cathy was like going "cold turkey." A month passed before he regained his old equanimity, once more engrossed in his research.

On a Tuesday in April, he returned to the library. The path along the brook was lined with fading daffodils, and tulips were about to unfold. He locked his bike to the rack, took his briefcase from the carrier, and walked to his usual alcove. Cathy was at her desk, speaking with another client. He took his notes from his briefcase and reviewed them.

A few minutes later, Jeff sensed that someone was standing to the right of his chair. He glanced up to see Cathy smiling at him. She was wearing his favorite dark brown dress with the large, round, white buttons down the front. "You haven't been here for a while. Have you been sick?" she inquired.

"Thank you for asking. I'm not sure I'd call it a sickness," he said vaguely, "but I'm fine."

She smiled warmly, "If you're better now, that's what counts."

Thrilled by her concern, he decided to advance his relationship. "You know, Cathy, you were a great help to me when I was getting started on my research and I'd like to show my appreciation by inviting you to lunch."

"That's very sweet of you," she replied with a smile. She glanced at her desk, where someone was waiting, and turned to go. "Maybe tomorrow at The Black Cat at noon?" she suggested, before hurrying back to her station. Stunned, Jeff was unable to reply until she was halfway back to her desk. For the next hour she was constantly busy. Jeff was so elated that he couldn't concentrate. Cathy was away from her desk helping another client when he finally prepared to leave. He tore a sheet of paper out of his notebook, addressed it to "Cathy W." on one side, and on the other wrote, "Noon tomorrow, The Black Cat—Jeff."

He folded the paper in half, so it stood like a tent, and placed it on Cathy's desk before leaving the library.

Jeff had a lot to think about in the twenty-four hours before their assignation. Her ready acceptance had shocked him. *Is she really fond of me? Does she imagine an intimate relationship? Is that what I really want?* As he looked in the mirror while he brushed his teeth that evening (after removing his denture), he saw a wrinkled face and unkempt gray hair. He reminded himself that he could no longer play tennis, dance, climb mountains, or make love.

Perhaps Cathy readily agreed to meet me because she could not imagine that I had anything but honorable intentions. When exactly, he wondered, *do the young think the old lose their lust? Am I nothing more than a dirty old man?* Jeff had to admit that when he was young, he thought sex between withered bodies was repugnant, imagining those withered bodies must have felt the same way. But in the youth-soaked, sex-stoked culture in which he lived, Jeff was not ready to admit he had reached that point of no return. His sexual capabilities had diminished while Lisa was still alive though. They would both start eagerly, but he was flaccid by the time she climaxed. "Is it not strange that desire should so many years outlive performance?" she once huskily quoted from *Henry IV* as they lay quietly afterward.

Jeff wondered whether a beautiful young woman would make love to an old fool who couldn't satisfy her when she had contemporaries who could. *Well, maybe there's more to love than sex. Could Cathy and I have a close relationship without sex?* He wasn't sure.

*

The entrance to The Black Cat, an upscale bistro a block away from the library, was bordered on three sides by low wooden planters with tulips surrounded by multi-colored pansies. A mid-morning shower had given way to scattered clouds, and lingering moisture filled the spring air with expectant freshness. When Jeff arrived, the waiters were setting small tables outside. He leaned his bicycle against the planter closest to the library, hung his helmet on the handlebar, and waited until the waiter had set the nearest table with a starched white tablecloth and service for two.

Jeff sat facing the library. Soon, Cathy approached, taking long confident strides, her leather bag slung over one shoulder and bouncing gently on her hip. This was the first time he had seen her outside the library. As he gazed at her admiringly, Jeff could not believe his fantasy was being fulfilled. He stood as she prepared to slide into the chair opposite him.

They were an unlikely pair. Cathy could have been mistaken for his daughter, or even his granddaughter. Pretty, with silken skin, regular white teeth, and clear green eyes, she was slightly taller than Jeff, carrying her slim figure very well. There was no mistaking Jeff's age: a bent five foot six, brow deeply furrowed, eyes rheumy at times, cheeks etched with lines; still, he had a full head of (gray) hair, spoke energetically, and could bicycle to the library and The Black Cat.

"I'm glad you picked an outside table," Cathy said, as the waiter poured their water and placed the menus on their plates. "It's so fresh and quiet out here."

"Quieter than inside I would imagine; we don't have to shout to hear each other. Do you eat here often?"

"No, I bring my lunch and eat in the staff

room, or in the park next to the library when the weather is nice. I can only afford this treat on special occasions, like today." (Jeff worried she'd think he expected her to pay for her lunch.) "I hope you're not superstitious?"

"You mean about black cats? No, not at all." On the contrary, Jeff thought it might be a good omen.

"Good," she laughed. "We're two of a kind." Her remark thrilled Jeff; his fantasy might be closer than he had imagined.

The waiter returned. "What will you have to drink?" They each ordered a glass of white wine. When the waiter brought the drinks, Cathy ordered soup and a tuna salad and Jeff a BLT with avocado.

"So, you are something of a mystery, Jeff. You're the only patron of your age who's working on a project as avidly as a graduate student working on her thesis. If you were on the faculty at the university, you'd be using its library instead of ours. So what do you do?"

Flattered by Cathy's interest, Jeff ran his hand through his hair, wondering where to begin, and where to end. "Well, I am a historian by training and when I was appointed headmaster at the Grove Academy"— Cathy nodded with familiarity—"I continued to teach American history until I retired. Knowing of my special interest, my eldest granddaughter gave me a new biography of Benjamin Franklin for my birthday last year." He didn't say how old he was. "Reading it rekindled my interest."

"In Benjamin Franklin?"

Jeff laughed. "I've been interested in Franklin since the fourth grade when I read *Ben and Me: A New and Astonishing Life of Benjamin Franklin as Written by His*

Good Mouse Amos."

"I know that book," Cathy interrupted. "It's in our Children's Section—by Robert Lawson."

Jeff ignored her interruption. "What mouse Amos did not say, and the new biography did—and what startled me—was that Franklin, fearing his imminent arrest, fled England in 1774, having been dismissed as deputy postmaster of the Crown."

"What crime did Franklin commit?"

"Advocating the removal of the anti-colonist governor of Massachusetts before King George's Privy Council—a crime in the eye of the Lords."

"That's fascinating," said Cathy, beginning her soup.

"Thanks to your help, I have discovered that this incident triggered considerable debate among historians as to whether Franklin's anger over losing his personal freedom sparked his hostility to the Crown, or whether it had been simmering for a long time."

"Fascinating," Cathy repeated as she finished her soup. "From your requests, I gather you've joined the debate."

"But I haven't taken sides." Cathy's salad and Jeff's BLT arrived. "Now it's your turn. Why'd you become a librarian?"

"I'm not sure I can give you a coherent answer. After graduating from university and taking temporary jobs for a few years, I joined the Peace Corps and spent two years in Rwanda teaching kids how to read. The kids' eagerness to learn built my confidence as a teacher. After the first year, I realized there weren't enough books to sustain the kids' interest and tried to establish a library and fill it with books and magazines that would attract them and advance their education. The administrative and practical obstacles were enormous, but I got a library off the ground and it continues to this day."

"Sounds pretty coherent to me," Jeff interrupted.

"When I got back to the States," Cathy continued, "I enrolled in a Library Sciences program, got my master's, and found a job as a librarian for a group of inner-city schools. If I thought the obstacles were considerable in Rwanda, they were much worse here. Besides, the kids here were much less motivated to read than the Rwandans. Many of them came from broken homes with single moms, some of whom could barely read themselves."

"There's only so much that formal education can do," Jeff interjected.

"I was impressed by the teachers in the schools I worked at, but two of those schools were closed because their pupils didn't do well on tests. That led to more overcrowding in the remaining schools, making matters worse."

"So, you burned out and took a job at a public library in a quiet middle class neighborhood?" Jeff gestured in the direction of the library.

Cathy's eyes flashed. "No! My position was terminated."

Lisa had often cautioned Jeff about interrupting. He felt embarrassed at what he had just said and annoyed that it could have diminished him in Cathy's eyes. "I'm sorry, Cathy. I should have let you finish."

"Thank you." She resumed her sandwich, chewing thoughtfully for a few moments. "Actually, my job is something of a cop-out. I have a few interesting patrons, like you," she smiled, "and I enjoy reading to kids—mostly lower middle class from families who have the time and inclination to bring them to the library." She put her sandwich down. "Besides, my boyfriend and I are trying to raise money to buy an abandoned store in the inner city and convert it into a library and small community center."

The word "boyfriend" stunned Jeff. He stared at Cathy, not hearing the rest of her sentence. "I'm sorry, I missed that last bit," he said. She repeated the sentence verbatim.

"Forgive me if I'm boring you, Jeff, I just feel so passionate about what we're doing." She looked at her watch. "Oh! My goodness! I should have been at my desk five minutes ago." She stood and reached for her pocketbook.

Jeff put his hand on top of hers and smiled, "It's my treat and I'd love to hear the rest of your story, and … and about your boyfriend, too. He must be really special to attract your attention."

"He is," she beamed. "I think you'd like him." As she turned to head back to work, she asked, "Will I see you at the library?"

"Not today, but later in the week."

"Good, then we can arrange to get together again. Thanks for lunch. Goodbye," she shouted over her shoulder.

*

"I guess you're not going to have dessert or coffee," the waiter said as he cleared away their plates.

"Wrong. I'll have a coffee, black," Jeff said, running his hand through his hair. "And bring the check."

Up until the moment she had mentioned her boyfriend, Cathy had kept Jeff's fantasy alive. That one word had instantly shattered it. As he sipped his coffee, he played back their conversation in his mind, including its abrupt end. Cathy had impressed him. *She's more committed to social justice than I was at her age—to the point of influencing her choice of profession. She never considered that I had an amorous interest in her, ascribing my inattention after she mentioned her boyfriend to boredom.*

He paid the check, got his bike and walked it past the planters, heading toward the library on his way home. At the library, he locked the bike to the rack but instead of entering the building he walked on the path alongside the brook, over a wooden footbridge. He thought about Cathy's boyfriend, his instant nemesis. He imagined him as young and muscular, attributes Jeff no longer had. *But what special trait could he have that attracted a woman as smart as Cathy? Could he also be intelligent?* He stopped to watch a three-year-old girl seemingly in conversation with one of the geese. Distressed that the goose would not answer, she reached her hand toward its beak, causing it to quickly flee and surprising the little girl. She looked at Jeff and began to cry. Her mother quickly approached, took the girl's hand, and walked away, scowling at Jeff. He circled back toward the library where he unlocked his bike and headed home.

Jeff wanted to continue his dialogue with Cathy, but the boyfriend loomed as an obstacle. His thoughts alternated between curiosity about the boyfriend and how he could continue to see Cathy. About halfway home, coasting down a slight hill, he got the idea to invite Cathy and her boyfriend to dinner. After Lisa had died, Jeff had improved his culinary skills, expanding his repertoire of dishes and gaining confidence in his ability. He began planning the menu and was so engrossed that he ignored a stop sign; a car halted abruptly, causing the irate driver to blare his horn at Jeff. Jeff pedaled blithely on and had the entire meal planned by the time he reached home.

On Thursday, Jeff visited the library and conveyed his plan to Cathy. "I'll have to check with Sean first. He has an erratic work schedule. Weekends might be better."

"No problem," Jeff replied. He gave her his e-mail address and phone number. He also established that Sean, her boyfriend, was not a meat eater but liked everything else, including fish; he modified the menu accordingly. Cathy e-mailed him the next day to say that Saturday a week hence would be perfect and offering to bring dessert. Relieved to have one less dish to prepare, Jeff accepted her offer, confirmed the date, gave her his address, and set the time for 6:30 p.m.

They arrived punctually. Cathy handed Jeff the box holding dessert and introduced Sean, who was not what Jeff had expected. Wearing a brown polo shirt, khaki slacks, and loafers, Sean was no taller than Jeff. He was muscular, with a rugged but not particularly handsome face, at least in Jeff's opinion, and thinning dark hair neatly combed back. Cathy, beautiful as ever, wore dark slacks, a short-sleeved, charcoal gray cashmere sweater, and flat sandals; dangling earrings were her only jewelry. Jeff ushered them into the living room and poured wine. "Excuse me for just a moment, I have to take the appetizer out of the fridge and put the veggies on the stove." He had prepared everything in advance and set the table, so he was gone no longer than a minute. When he returned, Cathy was holding a framed photograph of Lisa. "I knew your wife, Jeff."

"Really?" The photo had been on top of their baby grand piano for so long that he had forgotten it was there.

"She was the professor and chair of the Women's Studies Department at the university, wasn't she?" Jeff nodded. "I took a few courses with her when I was an undergrad. She was fantastic. A beautiful woman." After a moment's silence, Cathy added, "She must have left a great void."

Jeff ran his hand through his hair, not quite sure what to say. Finally, he agreed, "Yes, she's irreplaceable"—an idea he was only just beginning to accept. He poured himself a glass of white wine and sat on a rocking chair catty-corner to the sofa on which Cathy and Sean sat close to each other. "How did the two of you meet?" he asked.

They looked at each other. "Online," Cathy answered, "Match dot com"—an answer Jeff hadn't expected. Jeff had given some thought to match.com himself: "Eighty-year-old w.m. in good physical condition, seeks intimate relation with attractive young (under fifty) woman. Not interested in marriage." He never submitted it, certain that no woman would respond.

"You'd think you'd both have a wide open field among people you already knew. Why take a chance with someone you didn't?"

"You're wrong there, Jeff. Most people's field is pretty narrow—who they grew up with, went to college with, worked with. I never would have met Sean—he was too far out."

"Jeff has a point," Sean spoke for the first time. He had a deep, pleasant voice. "Cathy and I each tried many others—"

"—going on endless, boring dates," Cathy interrupted.

"—never coming close until we met each other," Sean finished the sentence.

"Although there was that cute guy from Buffalo," Cathy said with a smile, prompting a playful sock in the arm from Sean.

Jeff stood. "Let's eat. Please bring your wine glasses to the table." They followed him into the dining room, where he placed Cathy on one side of his seat at the round teak table and Jeff on the other.

"Ceviche!" exclaimed Cathy. "I first ate this in Mexico when I went with my sister a few years ago. Is it spicy?"

"Not too spicy, I hope," Jeff said, on his way to the kitchen to place the main course in the oven and fetch a basket of tortilla chips.

"Perfect!" they both exclaimed.

Jeff turned to Sean. "So, Sean, what did Cathy mean when she said you were 'too far out?'"

"Far out, and," Sean added, "far away. I only moved here after we met online."

"Let me put the 'far out' in context," Cathy interrupted. "I followed the conventional upper middle class route my parents expected—college, job, marriage. The Peace Corps broadened my horizons." She turned to Sean.

"I grew up halfway across the country in Detroit," he explained. "Neither of my parents went to college. Dad worked for GM and I did too, for ten years."

Jeff was amazed. His background was much like Cathy's; both his parents were college graduates and his father was a doctor. "I see what you mean, Sean. I would never have met anyone like you. Did you work on the assembly line?"

"Yes, the whole time. After a while, I could do my job and read at the same time. With a strong union, I made good money, but after a while I couldn't imagine doing the same work until retirement. When the plant closed, GM gave those of us with seniority the choice of one year's pay—about $60,000—or full tuition at an accredited college for four years plus a half year's pay."

"If I was in your shoes," Jeff said, "I'd have taken the tuition."

Cathy laid her fork down. "That's what Sean did, and that's one of the things that attracted me to him."

"Sounds like a no-brainer." Jeff got up to check the oven.

"Actually," Sean said, "out of four thousand workers laid off and given the choice, only ten took the tuition option."

Jeff stopped in his tracks. "That's astounding."

"When Sean told me, I was surprised, too." Cathy followed Jeff into the kitchen. "Can I help you with anything?" He handed her a basket of lightly toasted Tuscan bread and a shallow bowl of olive oil with a dash of Balsamic vinegar. He opened a chilled bottle of Sauvignon Blanc and brought it to the table. Cathy and Sean were talking. "Hold on, I want to pursue that four hundred to one ratio." A minute later, he returned carrying a casserole in his pot-holdered hands. He set the casserole on a trivet and with a flourish raised the glass lid, "Baked sea scallops in a nutmeg lemon butter sauce topped with breadcrumbs and parsley." He served them and then brought out a Caesar salad with cherry tomatoes, which he dressed at the table.

"Awesome," Cathy said after her first bite. They ate quietly for a minute or two.

"So, tell me, Sean," Jeff asked, "why did so many of your co-workers choose the $60,000?" He refilled their wine glasses.

Sean finished chewing and laid down his fork. "Well, first of all, most of them were older than me, often married and with kids, which had gobbled up their savings. Four years of college would stop the money coming in; they couldn't afford it. Others, married or not, were already in debt and saw the cash as a way out. A few were eager to improve their lifestyle—buy a boat, take a cruise or some other lush vacation." He picked up his fork.

"Seems pretty short-sighted to me," Jeff replied.

"That's the lifestyle they see on television every day," Cathy interjected. "'Why can't it be mine?' they ask.

"And go deeper into debt despite GM's handout," Sean answered. "My union runs classes on economics, trying to show workers how close to the poverty line they'll be at retirement unless they save. Pension plans are precarious and if they do pay out, they won't support an elegant lifestyle."

"So, you're a union man," Jeff commented.

"Third generation with the UAW. My grandfather walked the picket line with Walter Reuther in the 1930s."

"Sean's a union organizer now," Cathy said proudly.

"So that's what a college education's good for?" As soon as Jeff said this, he realized he sounded elitist. "I'm being facetious," he quickly added. "All these kids who become stockbrokers when they graduate will contribute a lot less to society than you will as an organizer."

"Yea!" shouted Cathy. "That's what I keep telling Sean." She turned to Jeff, "And as I told you at lunch a couple of weeks ago, we both use a good part of our spare time to help poor kids have a place where they can read and study." Jeff went to get another bottle of wine from the refrigerator.

They started to leave around ten o'clock. The conversation had drifted into more mundane topics, like where Jeff bought his fish and how he learned to cook. Cathy's homemade cherry pie was a great success. As they got up from the table, Jeff gently grasped Cathy's arm and said in a half-whisper, "I can see what attracted you to this guy." She bent slightly to hug Jeff and kiss him on the cheek.

*

Over the next year, Jeff, Cathy, and Sean had dinner together three or four times. Jeff continued to visit the library regularly and took Cathy out to lunch once or twice. He wrote a paper on Ben Franklin's run-in with the Privy Council. As part of his job with the union, Sean arranged classes for workers on various social, economic, and political topics. He invited Jeff to lead several classes on the American Revolution. After class, they'd go out and have a beer with some of the worker-students.

Jeff was best man at Sean and Cathy's wedding.

See Jane Run

"Jane, you forgot your water bottle," her mother yelled. Jane ran back to the car, grabbed the water bottle, slammed the car door shut, and waved perfunctorily to her mother and ran eagerly toward the opposite side of the main practice field at the university. Emelia, the Ramblers' patroness, watched ten-year-old Jane approach with long graceful strides, her face and blonde hair aglow in the descending sun, the jagged spires of the Organ Mountains behind her. "*Ella es una natural*," Emelia said to Juan, the team's coach. Juan's daughter, Maria, who was eleven years old, stood next to him. Emelia had been instrumental in organizing the succession of Ramblers' soccer teams when her daughters were even younger than Jane and Maria. Now they had scholarships at the university and played for the women's team, but Emelia retained a maternal interest in the Ramblers despite her other civic responsibilities.

Within minutes, ten other girls had been dropped off at practice. Seven of the girls were Hispanic and five were white, reflecting the population distribution of Las Cruces. Doug, the assistant coach, walked over from his faculty office on campus. Doug and Juan were both stocky; Juan had the look of a trim coach, Doug had a paunch and was bald.

"Good afternoon, girls," Juan shouted. "How are you all today?" The girls knew if they didn't shout, Juan would make them repeat their response, telling them they sounded "half-dead."

"*Bien,*" some shouted. Others shouted, "Fine."

"Are we going to beat the Marauders on Saturday?" Juan asked. The Marauders were a boys' team.

"*Sí,* Yes," they shouted back.

"OK. Let's begin with two laps around the field."

The girls took off. Lucy, Doug's daughter, and Jane started together. Lucy's pace was too slow for Jane, who soon shared the lead with Maria. Maria put on an extra burst but Jane quickly matched it, smiling at Maria as she appeared alongside her. A smile of camaraderie, not competition. Maria smiled back.

"You think the girls will be ready for the Marauders?" Emelia asked while the girls did their laps.

"If they're fired up, we'll beat them," Juan replied. "It's funny. You hear girls are spiteful, backbiting—more so than boys. Maria's not that way, and it's not true for the rest of the team either. They play more like a real team than boys at this age. They're not out there to be heroes; they cooperate. If they lack anything, it's aggression."

"You think they're afraid of getting hurt?" Emelia asked.

"No, we teach them body contact. They have their shin guards. They're more afraid of hurting someone than getting hurt, that's the problem. When they get fired up with team spirit, they're tougher."

"We've got to convey that the opposition is evil, undeserving of victory," Emelia commented. Juan and Doug looked at her with surprise. "That's how my teams over the years have won so many games."

"Winning isn't everything, Emelia," Doug replied, without looking at her.

Juan turned to look at Lucy trudging along with the pack. He kidded Doug, "What are you feeding Lucy? She needs more energy."

"She must have forgotten her PowerBar," Doug replied with a thin smile.

Jane and Maria finished their laps together, a minute before the pack. Emelia high-fived the girls, scolding the ones who brought up the rear. Although she did not know all their names, they knew she was the organizer of the Ramblers and their chief booster. Preparing to leave, she said loudly, "All right, girls, give it everything you've got. If you play well together, those nasty Marauders will be a pushover, and we'll clinch a place in the finals. Won't that be something!" Juan walked Emelia to her battered pickup truck before going on to his own truck, from which he pulled a large carton containing a half-dozen soccer balls and other paraphernalia.

He and Doug handed out the balls. The girls practiced dribbling footwork then passing back and forth using both feet. During the water break, the coaches put up portable goal nets at each end of the field and divided the girls into two squads, one slipping on blue jerseys that Juan distributed from his carton. Once when Jane was dribbling, Lucy, on the blue-jersey team, block-tackled her and got the ball away.

Jane could not keep her balance and fell. Lucy turned and helped her up. "Nice tackle, Lucy," Jane said.

*

The game against the Marauders was played on one of the grounds outside the Field of Dreams near Mayfield High School. With their portable chairs, Jane's parents joined the other parents from both teams. Like Doug, Jane's father, Stan, was on the university faculty. Again, the Organ Mountains—this time in sunlight at midday—were visible in the background. No trace remained of the previous day's winds that had tossed up sand and dust from the parched desert, obscuring not only the creosote bushes, mesquite, and cactuses but the mountains that ringed Mesilla Valley as well.

Neither team scored in the first half. At half time, Jane's father left his chair and with a few other dads listened to Juan as he analyzed the girls' efforts and told them they needed better teamwork, more passing.

In the second half, Juan assigned Maria to play forward and Jane midfield. Stan, tall and almost gaunt, followed the teams up and down the field from the sideline. Taciturn most of the time, he yelled encouragement to the Ramblers in his deep voice, calling the girls by name. When there was a clear opportunity to pass, he yelled to the player to send the ball to the midfielder or nearest forward. After six minutes of play, Jane received a pass and dribbled the ball up field until she could pass it to Maria, who trapped the ball and gave a strong strike with her laces that the goalkeeper could not block. The two girls hugged each other and quickly the rest of the team piled on. A cheer went up from the Rambler parents.

Two minutes later, the Marauders scored their

first goal.

Both teams tightened up their defense and the score remained 1–1 with one minute left to play. The Marauders gained possession of the ball and began to work toward the Ramblers' goal. Lucy was playing defensive back, and the Marauder forward was dribbling the ball toward her. Just as he entered the eighteen-yard box, Lucy stumbled and fell into the Marauder's path, bruising her cheek as she landed on the hard ground. Her body deflected the ball. The Marauder fell on top of her. He got up right away but immediately the whistle blew. "Foul," the referee called. Lucy lay on the ground for a moment as Juan and Doug ran toward her. The spectators became silent, as often happened when a player went down. "I tripped," Lucy shouted. "I didn't mean to fall."

"Penalty kick," the referee yelled.

A groan came from the Rambler parents. Some of them stood up and yelled almost in unison, "She tripped, she tripped."

Emelia arrived at that moment. She asked one of the parents who was still seated what had happened. "It was a tough call," the mother replied. "Lucy said she tripped. The referee didn't see it that way."

Juan and Doug walked Lucy off the field, washed her bloody cheek with water, and applied a sterile gauze dressing. Then Juan walked to the referee, protesting her call. The referee shook her head, positioned the ball twelve yards in front of the Ramblers' goal, and blew her whistle, signaling for the game to resume and the Marauder to take his shot. The Rambler goalie could not stop the ball from entering the netting, and the rest of the team could not score in the little time remaining.

As was customary at the end of a game, the parents of both sides formed parallel lines and all of the players ran between them, touching hands with the parents. After this ritual, the teams withdrew to separate parts of the field and had refreshments provided by a team parent. The Ramblers were sitting in a circle when Emelia stepped into the middle. "Who scored the goal?" she queried. Chatting around the periphery, the parents stopped to listen.

"Maria," Jane shouted.

"Nice going, Maria," Emelia continued. "Those Marauders were tougher than I expected." She turned to Lucy. "Too bad we had to throw away the game. You know the rules, Lucy. You should be ashamed of doing that."

No one spoke. Lucy got up and ran to her father, sunk her face into his side, and hugged him. As she sobbed, Doug stroked her hair. Embarrassed to silence by Emelia's remarks, the parents soon started to talk again and gathered up their kids to go home. Doug detached himself from his daughter and walked over to Emelia and Juan, who were getting ready to leave. "That's no way to talk to a ten-year-old, Emelia," he said angrily. "Certainly not in front of her teammates. You're not going to get better play from a child by ridiculing her. Besides, you took the referee's word for it. Lucy said she tripped, and it looked that way to me." Emelia opened her mouth to reply, but Doug continued, repeating what he had said at practice. "Winning isn't everything, Emelia. If Lucy wants to quit after what you said, I wouldn't blame her, and I'll quit coaching too. I'll form my own team." Both Juan's and Emelia's jaws dropped. Without waiting for a reply, Doug strode to his car with his arm around Lucy.

Jane and her dad heard the exchange. As they walked back to their car, Jane began to cry. She took Stan's hand. "What are you crying about, Jane? You played a great game; set Maria up perfectly for that goal."

Between sobs she said, "I don't want Lucy to leave the team. I'm afraid the team will break up."

"I hope you're wrong," Stan replied as he opened the rear car door for Jane.

Juan gathered up the team equipment and walked Emelia to her truck. "You shouldn't have said that, Emelia."

She stopped, turned, and faced him. "Said what?"

"Telling Lucy she should be ashamed of herself."

"You don't think she intentionally fell to stop him?"

"No, I don't, even though she's got the guts."

"I wanted that game badly, Juan. If we had won, we would have been in the finals and could have gotten regional standing. We did that when my oldest daughter was on the Ramblers and we went on to become state champions, which helped her get a scholarship at NMSU—the first Latina woman to do so." Almost at her truck, Emelia turned to look at Juan. "Of course, you know all that. Some of these kids will only go to college with scholarships. I want it for them as much as I wanted it for my kids."

"I know, but look, Emelia. You don't know these girls. They know you, though. They know what you've done. They respect you. When you come down hard on them, it hurts, really hurts."

"What do you want me to do?"

Juan did not answer right away. When they reached the cab of Emelia's old truck, he set down the carton of equipment. "I think you should apologize."

Emelia took a step backward. She put a hand on the cab door. "Apologize?"

"And you might think about putting in more of an appearance at our practices, too."

Emelia took the keys out of her purse. "Soccer isn't the only part of my public life, you know," she told Juan defensively. She started the engine and drove off. At home she told her two grown girls what had happened and asked what they thought she should do.

"Did you see Lucy fall?" the older one asked. No, she hadn't, Emelia replied.

"Then how do you know the referee was right?" the younger one asked. "We've seen them make plenty of mistakes."

"Should I apologize to Lucy and her dad?" It was a question a reprimanded daughter would more likely put to her mother than the other way around. Her daughters told her it was her decision.

*

After Emelia's criticism, Lucy was sure the team would blame their loss to the Marauders on her. Even Jane, her best friend, had not consoled her. Lucy's discomfort was reinforced by her father's angry rebuke to Emelia, with Juan standing nearby. Soccer and the Ramblers had become an important part of her life.

"Lucy's thinking of quitting the Ramblers," Doug said when they returned home after the game.

"Why? What happened?" her mother asked, looking at the bandage over Lucy's cheek. Doug summarized the situation, concluding with Emelia's accusation after the game. "Do you think," her mother asked, "if the girl who fell was Hispanic that Emelia would have yelled at her?"

The question had not occurred to Doug, but hearing his wife ask it riled him up. "That's it. I'm quitting." He looked at Lucy. "We'll start our own team, Lucy. How about that?" Lucy burst into tears and ran to her room.

Doug called Juan on Sunday evening and told him that he had had enough of Emelia's meddling in the team. "I'm quitting as your assistant and Lucy's thinking about leaving the Ramblers." He did not say he was thinking of starting his own team.

"I'm sorry to hear that, Doug. You know, after the game this afternoon I told Emelia that she had made a mistake and should apologize."

"What did she say?"

"She's thinking about it, I guess." Doug heard Juan cough over the phone. "Why don't you think over your position too, Doug. I'd hate to lose you as a coach."

"Okay, Juan, but I think it best if Lucy and I skip practice tomorrow."

After his call to Juan, Doug called Stan to tell him Lucy was very upset and might quit the Ramblers, and that he was about to give up his coaching position.

"That's too bad, Doug. The Ramblers are getting better with every game, partly with your help. They've had a winning season. Jane talks about nothing else. She's going to be very disappointed if Lucy leaves."

"My wife actually wondered if Emelia would have yelled at the girl who fell if she was Hispanic."

This speculation stunned Stan; it took almost a

minute before he answered, speaking slowly and deliberately. "You know, Doug, Jane's been on Rambler teams since she was six, longer than Lucy. Emelia was more active then, staying through most practices, even though her daughters had graduated to older teams. I often came early to pick up Jane and watch the team practice. Emelia was usually there, too, and I've seen both sides of her. She is tough—you know, the Vince Lombardi, winning-is-everything stuff—but she's also sensitive to the girls, white and Hispanic. She can soothe a six-year-old who's fallen or missed a kick better than anyone I know, including the girl's parents. Soccer for her is a way to help girls advance, Hispanic and white. So no, Doug, I don't think she'd treat a Hispanic girl any differently. I'm surprised your wife asked the question." He paused as Jane came into the kitchen. "Have you told Juan yet?"

"Yeah," Doug answered. "He said he told Emelia she should apologize."

"Well," Stan chuckled, "that sounds like Juan. Don't do anything rash, Doug. Take care."

Jane had washed and was in her pajamas. "Was that Lucy's dad?" she asked when Stan put the phone down. He nodded. "What did he say?"

"He told me Lucy's thinking of quitting the Ramblers."

"I hope she doesn't." She climbed onto Stan's lap. "I wanted to tell Lucy that I still loved her, that the penalty and our losing didn't make any difference, and I was sure the rest of the team felt the same way, but her dad took her away before I had the chance."

"I hope she doesn't, too." Stan got up, lifting Jane off his knee. "Come on, kiddo. It's time for bed. You've got school tomorrow."

*

Jane and Lucy didn't have a chance to talk until recess that Monday. They were on the playground, kicking a soccer ball around. "We're gonna miss you on the Ramblers," Jane told Lucy as she trapped the ball and stopped playing.

"How'd you know I was thinking of quitting?"

"Your dad spoke to mine last night."

"Really? I must have gone to bed already." She reflected for a moment. "Do you think he called up all the parents?"

"I don't know. I did hear my dad ask your father whether he had talked to Juan."

"What did he say?"

"I think from my dad's reply he had. Juan's pretty cool, isn't he? He treats us like grown-ups."

"Yeah," Lucy agreed.

"I hope you won't quit, Lucy. We need you."

"I'm not so sure. I'm not as fast as you are, Jane."

"But you pass well and you're not afraid to throw yourself in front of the ball or block."

"Are you talking about Saturday's game? I wasn't trying to foul or block him. I tripped."

"I know that. I saw you. No, I mean you don't seem to be scared out there."

"Sometimes I am. I'd rather play midfield than forward just because of that."

"Really?" Jane was surprised. "I cried when I heard your dad say he thought you might leave the team. I'll bet some of the other girls did, too." Jane reiterated, "We need you, Lucy."

"I really like playing with the Ramblers." Lucy paused. "My dad said something about forming a new team."

"I hope not. We've got a great team with you. Next year we'll get to the finals. I hope you're with us." The bell sounded and the playground emptied.

*

Lucy didn't show up for the Ramblers' practice that afternoon. Nor did Doug. Juan began with his ritual: "Good afternoon, girls. How are you all today?" Their answer was not as loud as usual, but he did not admonish them. He looked around, noting the absences. "Anybody know if Lucy is sick?" A lot of heads shook, "No."

Jane piped up, "I saw Lucy in school today. She's not sick. What Emelia said after the game really upset her. She must have felt like quitting."

"I'd feel like that, too," Maria said, looking at her father. The other girls chanted their agreement.

"Well, girls, if that's the way you feel, what are you going to do about it?" Juan asked.

"We should let Lucy know we want her to stay with the team," one of the Hispanic girls said. The rest of the team shouted their agreement and Jane was elected to tell Lucy.

*

Lucy skipped practice on Monday and moped around home that afternoon instead. "What's the matter, Lucy?" her mom asked.

"I have nothing to do. I miss soccer practice."

"Even after what Emelia said to you?"

"Emelia's not part of the team," Lucy replied. "She doesn't show up very often."

"Dad told me the other girls heard what Emelia said. Do you think they'll want you back?"

"Jane wants me back. We talked in school

today. She said the other girls do, too."

"Your father wants to start his own team. Wouldn't you like that?"

"He's not gonna get Jane. Maria's not gonna leave her dad. Jane and Maria are the Ramblers' best players."

"And you, too, dear."

Lucy didn't answer. She grabbed a soccer ball from her closet and went out to kick the ball around their patio.

With no coaching on Monday, Doug came home early while Lucy was outside. He listened as his wife reported her conversation with their daughter. "You know, dear, I don't want to ignite a culture war."

"You were provoked. You were defending your daughter."

"We could have talked it over calmly."

Lucy came in. "Hi dad."

"Mom tells me you were sorry not to go to the Ramblers' practice today. Do you want to rejoin the team?"

Lucy thought for a moment. "Yeah, those girls are my best friends and Emelia isn't our coach. I hope the team will take me back."

That evening, Jane called Lucy to tell her that the team voted unanimously to ask Lucy to come back. "I was elected to tell you."

The whole team showed up for practice Thursday. Doug was there, too. In response to Juan's opening question, the girls gave a resounding *"Bien*, fineT." The loudest ever.

*

Emelia watched the entire game the next Saturday. The Ramblers won 4–2. After the game, she stood outside the circle of girls as they had their refreshments. She walked up to Doug and took his arm. "I'm glad you're back, Doug. I don't know why it took me so long to realize that what I said to Lucy last week was out of bounds. I was invested more in winning games than in our players. I didn't see Lucy fall and had no business accepting the referee's call." Lucy stood alongside her dad. "I want to apologize to both of you."

Doug smiled as he turned to face Emelia. "I lost my temper, too. I'm just glad these girls are so cool."

"Lucy, you played very well last week, and today, too."

"We owe a lot to Juan," Doug said. "He understands the game, and the girls."

"Better than I do," Emelia replied.

One of the other parents came up. "Hey Emelia, I saw the new bumper sticker on your truck. Good luck."

"What's she talking about?" Doug asked.

Fishing her car keys out of her purse, Emelia smiled "I'm running for the Doña Ana County Board of Commissioners."

Doug smiled broadly. "You have my vote, Emelia."

The Umbrella

As Marvin was about to leave his old lab to meet Leslie's train, his wife called to ask about the tree. The crew had arrived to take it down and wanted to know whether they should split and stack the smaller limbs for firewood, which would cost an extra $100, or just grind them up.

"For the few times we build fires, it's not worth it," he told her. The tree, a giant oak, older than the American Revolution, had succumbed to the gypsy moth. Neither of them was happy to see it go.

Hurriedly, Marvin left the lab and drove down St. Paul, a gentrified street close to the station with stately brownstones and marble steps. He was lucky to find a metered parking spot. After calculating the cost if Leslie's train happened to be half an hour late, he dropped two quarters in the meter and headed to the station. He wondered whether he would regret inviting Leslie to Baltimore; they hadn't seen each other for fifty years. But the trees were beginning to blossom, the people he passed smiled at him, and the warm dry air eased his apprehension.

Every year since high school, Leslie had sent Marvin a birthday card. Marvin never remembered Leslie's and never thought to thank him until Leslie's most recent salutation came by e-mail for the first time. After the birthday wishes, Leslie had added, "Maybe we can get together before it's too late."

Marvin printed out the e-mail and propped it on the windowsill next to the cards from his family. He told Jean that he had gone to elementary and high school with Leslie. "You know, after all these years, I'm curious to see what he's like."

"Were you close friends?" his wife asked.

"Not in high school; I hardly ever ran into him."

"Maybe he remembers a lot of birthdays. A sort of hobby."

"I doubt it."

"You make it sound mysterious." Jean was a small, active woman whose brown hair had turned completely white while her cheeks remained ruddy and unlined. She was a teacher until the system required her retirement, but she kept busy by volunteering and painting with watercolors.

"We had a strange relationship."

"Well," Jean continued, "maybe you should see him. You need to keep busy now that you're retired. You'll soon wear out your welcome at your old lab, dear."

Although Marvin could easily have afforded the trip to New York, he invited Leslie to Baltimore. Leslie jumped at the chance. "I've wanted to see the Cone Collection at the Baltimore Museum of Art for some time," he replied. They agreed on a Tuesday in April and Marvin made a reservation for one o'clock at

Gertrude's, the restaurant in the museum. Knowing her husband's miserly bent, Jean counseled him to pay for Leslie's lunch. "Since you invited him, dear, and he's paying for his trip from New York, it would only be fair."

*

They had known each other since 1938, when their parents—second-generation American Jews whose parents had fled Russia—enrolled them in the same private elementary school in Brooklyn. Leslie relished being smart, striving to be the teacher's pet; Marvin couldn't have cared less. They went to and from school together, Leslie often trying to engage Marvin in some arcane detail of what they had learned, Marvin replying that the detail was pointless but making some point that had escaped Leslie. After school, Marvin played marbles or mumblety-peg in the earthen plots that edged the sidewalk in front of his house, or, when he was older, boxball on the sidewalk squares or stickball in the street, none of which Leslie was good at. Leslie practiced piano.

For one summer during the war, when both were eleven, they went to the same boys' camp in the Berkshires. Marvin and his other bunkmates, except Leslie, had been there before. They discovered that Leslie was afraid of daddy longlegs and delighted in dangling them before him and watching him squirm. Marvin joined in taunting Leslie and, by the end of the summer, led in devising plots to annoy his "friend." *Effete—a word I didn't know at the time,* Marvin reflected as he walked, *that's what Leslie was.* One of Marvin's friends called Leslie a fairy. When he found a daddy longlegs between his sheets, or even worse a small toad, he would scream piercingly. When Leslie did not return to camp the following summer, Marvin assumed it was because he could not endure the torture he and the other boys had inflicted.

They went to the same public high school in Brooklyn. In their first-semester honors English class, each proved nimble at writing and interpretation, but not as bright as Abe, tall and charismatic, whose literary skills exceeded theirs even though he came from a public elementary school. Abe recruited Marvin into the Sacco-Vanzetti Club, and while Marvin enjoyed singing revolutionary songs he found the club boring and soon quit. Leslie befriended Abe and a few weeks later Abe invited him to join the club. Marvin wondered whether Leslie was jealous that Abe had invited him first. By senior year, Leslie was the club's leader.

*

As he approached the station, Marvin wondered whether the stately marble columns were meant to instill confidence that the trains ran on time. If so, the enormous clock above the columns belied the possibility; it gave the correct time only twice in every twenty-four hours. The station's waiting room exuded senescence, with high-backed wooden benches a hundred years old, an uneven floor of the original pulverized marble, and dim light filtered through high, grimy windows. The information board clattered mechanically as a hidden agent kept it up to date announcing arrivals and departures. The train from New York was on time, due in five minutes. Leslie had said he'd be carrying an umbrella, but the balmy April morning was forecast to turn to showers, making Marvin doubt the umbrella would be a distinguishing feature.

No one resembling Leslie was among the first few passengers to sprint up the stairway from the track. That did not surprise Marvin. As a child, Leslie was roly-poly and clumsy. In the large mass of people filtering slowly through the double doors he finally saw a familiar face, rounded and smooth-shaven. The bald head gave him a moment of doubt, but the man was also carrying an umbrella. He was solidly built, now taller than Marvin, reinforcing the fact that Marvin had shrunk. Taking a chance, Marvin smiled at the man, who smiled back. Walking toward Marvin, the man shifted his umbrella to his left hand and held out his right. "Marvin?" The voice had not changed since high school. As they shook hands, Leslie hugged Marvin, who reciprocated weakly. "It's so good to see you after all these years!" Leslie exclaimed, with the same enthusiasm Marvin remembered.

"We have so much to catch up on," Leslie said as they walked to Marvin's car, but on the drive up Charles Street Leslie talked about his eagerness to see the Impressionist collection at the museum. He told Marvin that he had taken up painting and had even sold a few pieces. "Painting's a wonderful complement to music, Marvin."

"What exactly do you do with music?"

"I still play piano in a small chamber group." He reached into his small shoulder bag and pulled out a CD. "I brought you a recording of our group performing Beethoven's Archduke and the Brahms F minor quintet." He dropped it on the tray between the front seats.

Marvin was surprised that so few cars were in the museum's parking lot. Leslie was stunned by the grandeur of the museum, with broad steps leading up to a full-size copy of Rodin's Le Penseur, as well as Doric columns that supported the triangular pediment containing a classic Greek bas-relief. A guard informed them that the museum was closed on Tuesdays; only the restaurant was open.

"Don't worry about it," Leslie said. "We'll have more time to talk. I can always come down again."

Marvin winced. Had he made a mistake? "What time is your return train?"

Leslie pulled out his ticket. "4:47. That gives us over three hours."

They took an outside table, near the sculpture garden, even though clouds were gathering. The hostess asked Leslie if he'd like to check his umbrella. "No, it's very valuable; I prefer to keep it with me." After they were seated, Leslie immediately got up to go to the bathroom. "My prostate is not what it used to be," he smiled ruefully.

Marvin could not shake the idea that Leslie was planning to retaliate for the hurt he had inflicted at summer camp. He picked up the umbrella that Leslie had hooked over the back of his chair, tapping the barrel to check if it was hollow. Aiming the umbrella away from the table, he touched the trigger. It ballooned open instantly, right in front of the waiter who was bringing them water. The waiter took a step back, spilling water on his starched shirt. Marvin got up, "I'm terribly sorry. What a foolish thing to do. It's not my umbrella."

"That's all right," muttered the waiter, who was shaking the water off with a linen napkin as Leslie returned.

"What on earth happened?" he asked.

"Oh, I was examining your umbrella. It opened

accidentally." Leslie took it from Marvin, carefully rolling the black fabric around the stem and pushing it closed. "My mother gave it to me many years ago." He showed Marvin the curved wooden handle inlaid with mother-of-pearl. "The ribs are reinforced and the fabric is the finest silk."

The waiter rattled off the day's specials. "I'll give you gentlemen a few minutes to decide."

After the waiter retreated, Marvin pointed out that Maryland crab cakes were world renowned and particularly good at Gertrude's. On the menu they were listed with the annotation, "Market Price." Marvin echoed Jean's words. "Since you paid to visit me, Leslie, it's only fair that I pay for lunch. I'm afraid it doesn't match the train fare, but it's the least I can do."

"Thank you, Marvin." Leslie looked at his water glass. "Do you drink wine?" Not thinking about the cost, Marvin nodded.

"Well then, why don't we split a bottle? That might approach the fare, at least one way." They agreed on a $40 bottle of Sauvignon Blanc; Leslie ordered crab cakes and Marvin fried Chesapeake Bay oysters. Immediately after ordering, Marvin went to the men's room. He knew he was being paranoid, but he couldn't help fearing that Leslie might dissolve poison in his wine. He returned with wet hands just as the waiter was showing the bottle to Leslie, who nodded his approval, annoying Marvin; after all, he was paying for the wine. Leslie did the tasting and proclaimed the bottle satisfactory. "To the renewal of our friendship," Leslie toasted. The waiter produced a basket of crusty bread and a shallow dish of olive oil. Marvin broke off a piece and dipped it in the oil.

"You know Les, I thought I had earned your

eternal enmity through my behavior that summer at camp, playing all those nasty tricks on you to curry favor with the other boys."

Leslie laughed disarmingly, "That's what boys do." Then he frowned. "The snipe hunt was the worst. Leaving me in that rocky pasture above the camp on a moonless night to search alone for a bird you knew wasn't there. Stepping in cow flop and then losing my bearings; that scared me."

"I suppose that's why you didn't return to camp the next summer."

"No, that's not the reason, Marv. I wanted to come back to camp, a year older and a year wiser. But my parents couldn't afford it." Leslie poured them a second glass of wine. "That next summer in the city was miserable. My parents were afraid I'd get Polio and wouldn't let me go out. By not having to pay for camp, plus my scholarship, they were able to keep me in private school for the seventh and eighth grades."

"A scholarship? I didn't know they gave them for elementary school."

"I had learned to play the piano on an old, second-hand upright when I was three, and the school thought I was a prodigy."

Marvin the boy may have known Leslie's family was poor, but Marvin the man had forgotten; he regretted his harsh treatment and judgment of Leslie the child. "What did your father do?" he asked.

"He was a CPA, doing well at first. Then came the Depression and the few clients he had could barely pay for his services; he gave a lot of free advice. The year I was born he was able to get a second job as a shoe salesman and things got better. Still, without the scholarship they never could have started me in private school." Leslie dipped the last piece of crusty bread into the olive oil. "Dad gave up his second job when he developed arthritis, thinking he could manage as a CPA. But it became painful for him to use a mechanical adding machine and he couldn't afford an electric one. Some days he couldn't work at all. My mother took a job at an umbrella factory. Her mother, my grandma, moved in with us and took care of me while my mother worked."

Their entrées arrived, with julienne fries and a vegetable medley alongside the seafood. Leslie dug in. "You were right, Marv. These crab cakes are fabulous." They clinked glasses once again. Savoring the food, Leslie was silent for a few moments. "You know, Marv," he began, "I was jealous that your father was in the Army. He was in Okinawa, right?"

"At a station hospital behind the front. You have a remarkable memory, Les."

Marvin's father, a staunch anti-fascist and a doctor whose practice was beginning to flourish, was so enraged after Japan bombed Pearl Harbor that he volunteered for the U.S. Army Medical Corps in 1942. He had reluctantly agreed with his wife to send Marvin to private school, which they could scarcely afford. After the war, however, he insisted that Marvin go to public high school. Marvin, imbued with his father's radical zeal, heartily agreed.

"At summer camp in 1945," Leslie said, "when we heard about the A-bomb dropped on Hiroshima, I remember you saying, 'I guess I'll see my father soon.' I was really happy for you."

They continued to eat and drink silently until Marvin asked, "What did you do after high school?"

"I got accepted to Cornell on a New York

Regents Scholarship, but I couldn't go." Marvin waited for him to continue. "My father had to retire on disability. Thanks to Social Security we managed to scrape by, but it wasn't easy. My sister was born when I was a freshman in high school, an accident I suppose, and mom had to stop working; grandma was too frail to handle an infant. Very little money was coming in. We were almost evicted a couple of times. I got an after-school job as a soda jerk at Schrafft's on Flatbush Avenue when I was a junior; you wouldn't have known about that. In my senior year, my uncle wrote that he had gotten a job at the Ford assembly plant in Mahwah, New Jersey. I took a Trailways bus up there right after graduation, applied for a job, passed my physical, moved in with my aunt and uncle, and started on the line dropping pistons into cylinder blocks for Fords, Mercurys, and later Edsels."

"I've never been inside a factory," Marvin admitted.

"It's awesome at first, but you're not missing much. Even if the air hadn't been hazy under the fluorescent lights, with sparks flying from the welding guns, you wouldn't be able to see the end of the line. So noisy you couldn't hear yourself talk; they made us wear earmuffs, very unpleasant in the summer. I started on pistons 'cause they weren't heavy. I hadn't been athletic in school—"

Marvin interjected, "I remember."

"—and I was pretty weak. After a year I was able to handle a welding gun, firing it as the chassis rolled by one after another. That got me a raise to $3.10 an hour, real good in those days. At the Sacco-Vanzetti Club we talked a lot about class struggle and capitalist exploitation; now I was witnessing it. Of course, I joined the UAW right away. The men elected me shop steward and I got a reputation as a successful grievance negotiator with the men in ties and white shirts."

Marvin felt like crawling under the table, embarrassed that he had misjudged Leslie. He had always considered himself progressive, if not radical, having participated in left-wing organizations in college and graduate school. Some of his friends had volunteered for the fateful Mississippi Freedom Summer Project in 1964. By that time, he had married Jean, had two kids, secured a faculty appointment in biochemistry, and purchased a modest house on the outskirts of Baltimore. He had joined the March on Washington in 1963, participated in anti-Vietnam War demonstrations later in the sixties, and given money to progressive causes, but it was fluff compared to Leslie's existential involvement with capitalism. Marvin came to believe that his research was too esoteric to have any redeeming social value.

The waiter cleared the table and they ordered coffee. While they lingered, the waiter brought the bill. Marvin looked it over and placed his credit card in the leather folder in which it came. After the waiter refilled their cups, picked up the folder, and left, Marvin asked, "Why were you so eager to get together, Leslie?"

Picking up his cup, Leslie took a few moments to answer. "You were my idol at school. You never seemed to study but you always knew the answers. I never remember you crying, even in kindergarten; I cried a lot. I envied your athletic prowess and you were—," he hesitated, "—handsome." He placed his cup in the saucer. "In modern parlance, you were cool."

Marvin grimaced. "You know, being a cool kid

can be a curse."

Leslie expressed surprise.

"Private school was easy. My teachers and my parents kept telling me I was smart. When I got to high school and discovered there were kids like Abe who were much smarter without the benefit of private school, I began to doubt how smart I was. I almost flunked out of college. And my scientific insight is nowhere near Nobel Prize caliber; dabbling, you might call it."

"But you were successful. I've read about your work in the newspapers. You served on national committees. I saw you once on Nova."

Marvin no longer thought these accomplishments important. His research filled in details; it wasn't groundbreaking. He hadn't changed public policy. He hadn't, to his thinking, inspired students. He hadn't gotten his hands dirty. "I'll tell you, Leslie, the most satisfying thing I ever did was protest the Vietnam War." He quickly added, "I'm sure you did, too, but what I did pales in comparison to using your hands to make a living."

He signed the bill and returned the credit card to his wallet, then guided Leslie on a quick tour around the sculpture garden. They continued to talk on a wrought iron bench while clouds gathered and a damp coolness settled over the garden.

"How long did you stay with Ford?"

"Ten years. After you master the repetitive motions, your mind wanders. I began to think about playing the piano. Ford started to lay off workers as the economy sagged; the Edsel was a bust. I had sent home enough to help my parents out until my mother was able to go back to work when my sister started school.

Mom pleaded with me to quit; she didn't want to see her aspirations for me swallowed by the assembly line. I moved back with my parents, rented a piano. With all that welding, my fingers weren't as nimble as they used to be, but I was competent and studied theory on my own. The admissions committee at Julliard liked my commitment and was impressed by my blue-collar experience; academics always seem surprised when someone who's worked on an assembly line shows some culture. I got a bachelor's degree in music after five years, working part time; met Gloria, my future wife, who was studying dance at Julliard; and got a job teaching at the School for the Arts, playing chamber music on the side. We have three kids and four grandchildren," Leslie beamed. "I try to keep in shape to keep up with them."

Carrying an umbrella, their waiter approached. "You might need this today," the waiter said.

Leslie was shocked. "I've never lost this before. It's very dear to me." He offered a couple of dollars to the waiter, who refused the gesture. Marvin glanced at his watch. "Four o'clock, Leslie. If we leave now, we can beat the rush hour and you won't have to worry about missing your train." They headed back to the parking lot.

In ten minutes, they were back at the station. "Why don't you drop me?" Leslie asked. "I don't mind waiting for half an hour."

"No," Marvin replied. "I'll park and walk you."

He was not so lucky with parking this time, finally finding a spot on East Lanvale, four blocks from the station. Many of the houses on the block were boarded; garbage cluttered the sidewalk. Heralding the storm, a gust of wind swept through, tossing the garbage a few inches, rattling empty soda and beer cans scattered along the curb as the sky darkened. Heading toward the station, they paid scant attention to a kid they passed who was wearing a dirty sweatshirt, its hood wrapped tightly around his head. As they stopped to cross Charles Street, Marvin felt a gun in his back and an adolescent voice piped up, "Gimme your wallets and there won't be any trouble." Marvin broke into a cold sweat as he felt the kid probe for his wallet. The youth lowered his gun as he opened the wallet. At that moment, Leslie, who had been watching carefully, swung his umbrella upward at the pistol, tossing it into the air. The boy started to run. Leslie chased him but the youth was too fast and escaped down an alley. Marvin seemed glued to the spot. When Leslie returned, Marvin was trembling, feeling his empty back pocket. Leslie found the weapon a few feet away, next to some empty garbage cans. Thinking about fingerprints, he pulled out his handkerchief to pick it up. "I'll be damned," he said. "A toy cap pistol. Some nerve that kid had."

Still trembling, Marvin said, "I could have been killed, Leslie. You took a big risk, hitting him with your umbrella. If it was a real gun, I could be lying on the sidewalk bleeding to death." Again, it flashed through his head that maybe Leslie had come to kill him.

"I watched the kid closely, Marvin. He lowered his pistol when he flipped open your wallet. That's when I struck." He put his arm around Marvin. "Let's go back to the car so you can drive me to the station, where we can report the theft to the police—they usually hang out near train stations—and give them this 'deadly' weapon." He brandished the pistol through the handkerchief.

"But I can't drive without my license."

"Under the circumstances and with the pistol as evidence, the police will understand." They retraced their steps, walking across the entrance of the alley into which the thief had disappeared. Leslie noticed a flat tan object lying in the middle of the alley. "Wait here," he said to Marvin, as he quickly walked ten yards to retrieve the object. He handed it to Marvin.

"My wallet!" Marvin exclaimed. He opened it and found his driver's license and credit cards. "Forty bucks, that's what he got."

"He didn't want to get caught with the wallet; he tossed it as fast as he could."

Marvin parked in a passenger-loading zone in front of the station; Leslie got out and returned with a policeman. He handed the pistol to the cop, explaining what had happened. "I've got a train to catch, Officer. My friend here, he's the one who was robbed." Marvin had gotten out of the car, and Leslie gave him a hug. "Thanks for a lively afternoon, Marvin. Next time, maybe you'll come to New York." Swinging his umbrella, he disappeared into the station.

Marvin filled out a form for the police and drove home. Jean greeted him. "How did it go?"

"Not exactly what I expected."

He described the mugging. "While I stood there paralyzed, Leslie sprang into action."

Jean put her arms around him. "That was a dangerous thing for Leslie to have done."

"I was dead wrong about Leslie," Marvin told her. "He's changed completely and done more with his life than I've done with mine."

"Let's not start that again," Jean muttered.

"In high school, getting a job was not on my

radar. Leslie had to work part time and then had to support his parents. Couldn't go to college. Worked on a Ford assembly line and was an organizer for the UAW." Jean looked impressed. "And then, he paused, went out to his car, and returned. "And then," he waved the CD in front of Jean, "he got a bachelor's degree, became a teacher and a pianist good enough to make recordings."

"Maybe you should lie down," Jean suggested.

"That's what I've been doing all my life." He walked out to their backyard through the sliding patio doors and then came in a minute later. "The tree's gone. The lawn looks naked."

"It's awful without it, isn't it? That tree was an important part of our lives: the kids climbed it; you threw a rope over one of the lower limbs so they could swing from it."

"Yeah, and raking its leaves was a family ritual at Thanksgiving." Marvin paused for a moment. "Maybe we should have saved the smaller limbs."

Jean hugged him. "I did," she whispered. "They're piled alongside the shed."

Marvin released her arms. "For $100?" he asked angrily.

Again, she put her arms around him. "Only ten. They just stacked the logs. I thought it might be good for you to split them."

Marvin smiled, hugged and kissed his wife, descended the basement stairs, pulled out a long-handled axe that had lain unused alongside his workbench, and sharpened it on a hand-cranked grindstone wheel. Holding the axe at its throat, blade down, he walked outside to the shed against which the logs were piled. Thunder rolled ominously and the young leaves trembled, but it did not rain.

Marvin picked up a log and set it upright on an old, flat stump. He hadn't swung an axe for many years but thought he remembered the motion. His first blow barely nicked the log, which simply toppled over intact. He thought for a moment, went back to the basement, and returned with a wedge. His next blow was not as violent as the first; better aimed, it succeeded in cracking the log. He placed the wedge in the crack, stood up, rotated the axe handle, and struck the wedge with the blunt side of the blade. The log split cleanly and Marvin started a pile with the two halves. He soon developed a rhythm as he split one log after another, almost like an assembly line. What had Leslie told him? *After a year I was able to handle a welding gun ... successful grievance negotiator with the men in ties and white shirts.* Marvin began to sweat. *That's me, the man with the tie and white shirt*, he thought as he brought the axe down. He split twenty logs before the blisters on both hands started to ooze, making the axe handle slippery and the pain intolerable. Feeling better though, he went inside and washed up for dinner.

A Cascading Failure

The greatest threat to the security and reliability
of our electrical infrastructure is foliage…
—G. Bakke, *The Grid*, 2016, p. 122

The electrical resistance of a power line causes
it to produce more heat as the current it carries
increase…Automatic protective   relays detect
the   excessively   high   current   and   quickly
disconnect the line, with the load previously
carried by the line transferred to other lines. If
the   other   lines   do   not   have   enough   spare
capacity to accommodate the extra current
their overload protection will react as well,
causing a cascading failure.—
https://en.wikipedia.org/wiki/Northeast_bla
ckout_of_2003

At first, the power blackout was unexceptional; major
outages had occurred with increasing frequency over
the previous thirty years. The early ones were due to
lightning, earthquakes, faulty equipment, and human

error. But since 2000 an increasing proportion had been due to climate change—both directly, caused by unprecedentedly violent tornados and hurricanes; and indirectly, as global warming accentuated by sweltering heat waves overtaxed the electrical grid, the interlocking source of electricity for the country. That is what happened on Thursday August 28th, 2023.

Extreme hot weather across most of the country had increased demand for air conditioning and other types of refrigeration, and for water, which had to be pumped for household, commercial, and agricultural use. Meeting this demand caused power lines to overheat and lengthen as they began to carry more current than they were designed to hold. Sagging high-voltage lines in New Jersey, Missouri, and Utah arced as they touched the foliage below them causing local bursts of lightning-like electricity, shorting out the lines, and shutting down service to houses, businesses, and farms. In Utah, one short circuit ignited a forest fire. The electricity that each of these shorted lines had carried was now shunted to other lines. Already operating close to capacity, these lines also overheated, sagged, and shorted out. In turn, the electricity they had carried was shunted to other, still-functioning lines that also shorted out. In a matter of minutes, the entire nation and adjacent swaths of Canada and Mexico were without electricity.

The outage began at 5:12 p.m., EDT. With the whole country in sunlight, people outside were not immediately aware that something had gone wrong. Then rush hour traffic on the east coast quickly backed up when traffic lights stopped functioning. Police were dispatched to the most congested roads until even the supply of off-duty police was exhausted. Traffic jams occurred across the country as the afternoon advanced westward.

For the first few days, emergency generators kept radio and television stations going, Internet servers operating, and newspapers publishing. Uncertain whether the outage was a terrorist attack or a natural disaster, the Department of Homeland Security issued a red alert which interrupted regularly scheduled programs at 5:30 p.m., EDT:

> A power outage affecting the United States and parts of Canada and Mexico started today at 5:12 p.m., EDT. Until the reason for this outage has been established, we cannot estimate how long the blackout will last. Laptops, mobile phones, electric vehicles, and other devices that run on electricity will not operate when their batteries are depleted unless they are attached to a back-up generator. The public is advised to stock up on food and water, use existing supplies sparingly, and open refrigerators as little as possible.

Most homes did not have back-up generators. In those with charcoal or gas grills, or with stoves fired by natural gas, propane, or wood, cooking was still possible. Homes with electric stoves made do with leftovers, salads, or delicatessen. People across the country ate supper in natural twilight.

As dusk faded into darkness, the streetlamps did not come on. Young children accustomed to night lights cried mightily in the pitch dark. On the horizon, there was no glow from illuminated parking lots or sports stadiums. Where twinkling lights had once indicated the presence of civilization, there were only black holes. On Friday morning, lines formed at supermarkets and drugstores for food, bottled water, flashlight batteries, candles, and other necessities. In stores without generators only cash was accepted; ATMs and credit cards were worthless. A run on banks for cash withdrawals ended only when a bank's reserves or its back-up generator ran out.

*

After leveling off, electricity consumption had started to rise in 2019 as the increasing use of bitcoin currency put new pressure on the grid. Bitcoin miners needed an extraordinary amount of electricity to generate the necessary computing power to find the randomly generated numbers that were key to their wealth. Some small cities had banned them because they were consuming most of the city's electricity. In 2018, Bitcoin had used as much electricity as the entire Czech Republic.

In 2021, the newly elected Democratic Congress had passed legislation that raised the gas efficiency of cars to seventy-five miles per gallon. It also had provided tax credits to buyers of electric vehicles, stimulating demand and further increasing consumption of electricity.

Alternative sources of electricity—solar and wind—were able to shunt the surplus energy they generated into the grid. Regional grids amalgamated, leading by 2022 to one national grid. This worked fine, except on extremely hot days when it didn't.

After sunset and when the wind diminished, solar panels and wind turbines could neither generate nor store electricity. The country then relied on electricity generated by coal, natural gas, nuclear reactors, and water, all distributed through the grid. Coal was a major contributor to climate change and was being phased out. Natural gas, made cheaper by environmentally harmful fracking, also contributed to climate change. Rusting dangerously, nuclear power plants threatened to melt down, spewing radioactivity over the countryside, as with Chernobyl in 1986. Many nuclear plants had been decommissioned and were not replaced. Hydroelectric dams, less harmful than these other sources, had not always been adequately maintained.

In part to meet the shortcomings of solar and wind power, research and development of batteries to store excess electricity had increased. New technology enabled electric cars that were not in use to supply power to the homes where they were charged, but no major breakthroughs had come by 2023 when the blackout stopped much of the R&D.

There was no evidence that terrorist hackers had shut down the grid on August 28th. Investigative journalists still on the job discovered that many of the trees touched by the overloaded, sagging power lines had been scheduled for trimming or removal by public utility companies. Facing competition from solar and wind power, the profits of these companies depended on how cheaply they could distribute electricity; one way to save money was to lay off the workers who maintained the power lines. The number of trees that the smaller workforce could trim or remove in a given time was reduced, but the trees did not stop growing and the backlog in need of maintenance increased. Burying electric wires underground, thereby reducing the problem of arcing with trees, proved too expensive to be profitable.

*

The grid was still down across the nation on October

1st. By then, radio and television stations were forced to broadcast only emergency announcements at pre-specified times in order to conserve fuel for their back-up generators.

At supermarkets across the country, storefronts were plastered with notices of the last sales, but inside the shelves were bare and the aisles deserted. Rats and other vermin had consumed the few fruits, vegetables, and meats that had not been bought. Lacking refrigeration, cartons of milk turned sour, butter rancid, and eggs sulfurous.

Signs announcing regular gas at $3.99 per gallon swayed in the breeze, but no cars lined up in front of the useless pumps.

With limited markets for their goods, appliance stores stood unharmed. Only the liquor and drug stores, their windows and gates smashed, had been looted.

Garbage collection had ceased, and sewage systems had started to back up.

Mobile phones, many of them plugged expectantly into worthless wall sockets, no longer supported a vast amount of social intercourse. With nothing else to do after dark another form of intercourse had flourished, as became evident nine months later.

*

The days passed. Gentle breezes rustled the leaves, birds trilled in the morning, crickets chattered on warm afternoons and into the evenings, and thunderclouds emitted sound and light spectacles at night. But there was no hum of automobiles or rattle of trucks; no slamming of car doors; no sirens from ambulances, fire engines, or police cars; no train whistles; no drone of airplanes; no blare of radios or televisions. Gloomy evenings, illuminated only by flickering candles. Laughter, voices, and even babies' cries were subdued.

*

Twenty-three named hurricanes had already occurred in 2023 so the storm brewing in the Gulf of Mexico on October 3rd was named Xerxes. With the grid still down, the National Weather Service did not have the capability to track it as fully as previous storms. The storm made landfall in the United States in Mobile, Alabama, as a Category 5 with winds up to 200 miles per hour. It cut a swath through Alabama, Tennessee, turned north-east through Kentucky and Ohio, and then diminished into a tropical storm over Lake Erie. Xerxes was the second proverbial "one–two punch" to the grid, adding new damage as wind and trees knocked down more power lines, which would need to be repaired before electricity could be restored.

The hurricane trapped most people in their homes; without electricity, evacuation centers had few volunteers or food. Hospitals that had lost their back-up power had fewer admissions and only skeleton staffs to attend them. Had someone been counting, they would have found that the death toll from wind and flooding had reached a record high.

Out west, the power failure had reduced the risk of fires ignited by falling wires, but forests and fields, many abutting towns and small cities, were still prey to natural and other sources of man-made fire. In October, fires along the west coast spread to Idaho, Nevada, Utah, and Arizona and could not be contained because of difficulty getting firefighters and equipment, as well as water, to the fringes of the fires. People in adjacent towns could only flee by foot or bicycle, leaving all but their smallest possessions behind. Many did not escape. Smoke hung over Phoenix, Los Angeles, San Francisco, Las Vegas, and Salt Lake City. Deaths from asthma and emphysema more than doubled. Eventually, the fires burned themselves out or were doused by rain, or by snow at higher elevations.

*

As autumn progressed, the trees lost their leaves, covering sidewalks and clogging sewer drains in cities and towns with their yellow, red, and brown detritus. Night-time temperatures in many parts of the country fell below freezing, and people began to worry about surviving the winter. Where would their heat come from? Where would their food come from?

Those living on farms were better off. Farmers rebuilt old horse-drawn wagons to haul their surplus vegetables to starving small towns nearby after harvest. If they had saved seeds for planting, chopped wood to burn in stoves and fireplaces, kept wells clean and sewage lines cleared, all of which they were accustomed to doing, they would be more likely than their urban counterparts to survive the blackout.

By January, snow was several feet high on northern roads untrammeled by plows. Torn away by the weight of snow and ice, gutters dangled worthlessly. Some roofs collapsed.

Homeless people who could not find shelter were among the first to die. Frail elderly in heatless nursing homes and assisted living facilities were next. Infants and young children fell victim to malnutrition, starvation, and death. Well water, snow saved in cisterns and buckets, and occasional rain staved off death from dehydration, but more so in rural and suburban areas than inner cities.

Death rates from addictive drugs decreased as they could no longer be bought at any price. Despair became endemic; suicides increased, and hopelessness led to slower deaths in unkempt homes thick with dust, dirty dishes, unmade beds, and overflowing garbage. Rats scurried back and forth mutilating human bodies.

When the days grew longer, the snow melted. Water pooled in the streets, flooding lawns and basements. Diseases like cholera, which had disappeared in most communities, reappeared in epidemic proportions. Pernicious ivy crept up outside walls, kudzu strangled shrubbery, and gray mold took hold on damp surfaces inside. Weeds split the sidewalks, driveways, streets, and roads. Potholes turned into small craters. Half-filled swimming pools became slimy green with algae.

On sunny days the sky was cobalt blue, free of smog from automobiles and upwind factories whose furnaces no longer burned. Daffodils came up, followed by tulips. With hand lawn mowers a relic, grass on playing fields was chest high by July, making them unusable for the few resilient young people still able to play. Roses, carefully tended before, bloomed chaotically as few people had the inclination to prune them; petals paled, lost their turgor, and fell lifelessly to the ground.

Without transportation and with insufficient land and labor, burials became a problem. As the death toll mounted, bodies left to decay in the streets created a new source of disease. Some communities dug mass burial graves; others performed mass cremation on wooden funeral pyres, the stench of burnt flesh hovered over their towns.

Isolated enclaves with their own microgrids powered by solar and wind energy had electricity at least part of the time and became targets of envious surrounding populations. Protected more by their own militia than by the police or military, these enclaves engaged in bloody battles with outsiders who tried to invade and occupy their homes. The death toll increased further, and in the crossfire many of the microgrids were destroyed.

*

Accustomed to cheap electricity at the flip of a switch, people had become less resourceful during the twentieth century, especially in large cities. The profoundly destructive cascading of overheated power lines left surviving Americans so dazed that among the survivors—still numbering in the millions spread across the country—few had the wherewithal to restore the grid or develop replacements.

Other countries that were not affected by the blackout debated giving assistance—a reversal of the Marshall Plan that had revived Western Europe after World War II. But the governments of Europe offered minimal help, paralyzed by extreme nationalists on the right and revolutionaries on the left. Elsewhere, schemes were being hatched to invade the defenseless United States and seize its natural resources, including vast amounts of fertile land, creating a vassal state.

One thing is certain: The collapse of the North American grid stemmed the rise in global temperatures that threatened the entire earth. If it was the only solution to climate change, some countries were in no hurry to help.

Brahms' Fourth Symphony

"I've come about Michael Silver," she told the officer at the desk. He asked her name, looked at his register, buzzed an inner office, and told her to take a seat. A few minutes later, a good-looking woman in her forties with close-cropped brown hair, wearing a pale blue shirt, a solid tie, and deep-blue trousers, approached and held out her hand. "Molly Mitchell, Dr. Greenfield. Thank you for coming in. Please follow me." When they were both comfortably seated, Mitchell opened the folder on her desk. "The trooper who visited you this morning reported that you had spoken with Professor Silver after his lecture last night." She looked at Joan to confirm.

"Yes, I asked him a question when he finished speaking. We spoke some more at the reception afterwards."

"Do you go to many lectures at the college?"

"Actually, Professor Silver's was the first one since my husband died two years ago."

"Was there something special about Professor Silver's lecture?"

"Well, it had sparked a lot of controversy. The student nominating committee chose Silver as the Hooper lecturer. He had discovered that health problems near a chemical plant owned by the Hooper family resulted from the plant's run-off. The Hoopers threatened to withdraw support for the college if Silver spoke, but the students refused to withdraw Michael's nomination and the controversy spread beyond the campus, garnering bad press for the Hoopers. At the last minute, the Hoopers bowed to the students' protest and withdrew their threat."

"Michael?"

"Professor Silver."

"Did you know Professor Silver?"

"We met forty years ago. I hadn't seen or heard from him since."

Mitchell looked at the folder again. "Did Professor Silver seem intoxicated after the lecture?"

"Not in the least."

"Did he drink at the reception?"

"They only served wine. He may have had a glass."

"His blood alcohol content was 0.26 percent in the emergency room, over three times the safe limit. Do you have any idea how he became intoxicated?"

"Yes. That's why I came in." Mitchell looked at Joan expectantly. "It's a long story."

"I have plenty of time," Mitchell replied.

"I'm so glad you're a woman. Do you mind if I call you Molly?"

"Not at all."

"I've never told the whole story to anyone, not even Donald, my late husband."

*

I had last seen Michael when he was eighteen and I was twenty-nine. The announcement that he would give the Hooper lecture blew dust off the memories in the attic of my mind. I played out scenarios that had never happened and never could have happened. At first, I thought I wouldn't attend but as the day approached and what had happened consumed me, I realized I had to go. Vanity got the better of me and I spent time brushing my hair, tying it back in a chignon, applying rouge to perk up my lusterless face, and finally lipstick. Still the same slim five feet, though slightly bent, I chose a black dress, its hemline just above my knees, almost identical to the one I wore when I visited Michael and his parents forty years ago. Not since Donald was alive had I worn makeup or dressed up.

Anticipating that the hall would be packed, despite a late winter storm warning in effect for northern New England, I left plenty of time to park and walk to the lecture hall. By the time I reached it, snow was falling heavily, covering the walkways and grassy areas and muting the voices of people converging and the sounds of cars streaming by. Several faculty friends of Donald greeted me and felt obliged to talk. I brushed them off politely so I could get a seat up front.

Michael seemed less scrawny. Perhaps it was his sports coat—attire I hadn't seen him in before. His face was more rounded, though still smooth—unlined, boyishly beardless. He began by thanking the college for inviting him and then turned to the Hooper heiress and thanked the family for sponsoring his lectureship despite "some differences of opinion." The audience applauded and the heiress's smile and gracious wave of her hand acknowledged his olive branch. Michael's lecture recounted how his laboratory had tied the epidemic of birth defects and malignancies in nearby families to the chemicals discharged from the Hooper plant.

I paid close attention to his talk so I could ask something intelligent in the customary question period at the end of his talk. Not that I had anything burning to say, I just wanted to see if he'd recognize me.

After the first flurry of questions, I walked to the floor microphone and waited for him to point in my direction. "You have shown," I began, "how science can be used to discover the effects of the environment on people's health, but you haven't talked about how such pollution can be prevented."

Michael did not seem phased. "An excellent question uh, uh—" I thought he was going to address me by name. But I doubted he knew my married name, or even if I had been married. To have called me Joan, or even Dr. Greenfield, might have raised eyebrows. Or was the "uh, uh" simply hesitation while he formulated his answer? "That's really another lecture," he started. "But let me say that the federal government has set up a National Toxicology Program to study harmful effects of commercial chemicals, and Congress has established a superfund to clean up hazardous sites. I'd be pleased to discuss this with you further at the reception." He hadn't offered that to any of the other questioners. "And, oh yes—," he added before calling on the next person, "I am donating my entire honorarium for this lecture to the Environmental Defense Fund." Again, there was applause. This time the heiress did not smile.

Mitchell tapped her pencil, seemingly impatient.

"Sorry I'm taking so long to tell this story, Molly. I don't want to leave anything out."

Students and faculty were gathered around Michael by the time I reached the reception so I filled my plate with canapés and chatted with some old friends while keeping an eye on him. When the cluster around him dissolved, he scanned the room and approached. "Joan!" We hugged politely. "You look great—the same slim figure you had at Camp Whitebirch, the last time I saw you. The same throaty voice." It was probably my voice he recognized, nothing else.

"No," I reminded him. "The last time was dinner at your parents' apartment in Manhattan, a few weeks after camp ended. You left before dessert."

Michael's father had invited me to dinner. He was a physician at the hospital where I was a fellow in pediatrics. Passing me in the corridor one morning in September, he stopped to thank me for taking care of Mike's asthma at camp. "You look like you could use a home-cooked meal. Why don't you join us for dinner tonight?" I wasn't feeling well and told him I'd let him know in the afternoon. "I hope you'll join us," he said sincerely. "I'll check with Evelyn to make sure it's OK. Mike's leaving for college next week, you know. I'm sure he'll be happy to see you before he goes." I smiled wanly and thanked him. Later that day I felt better—even hungry—but still wasn't sure dining with the Silvers was the right thing to do. About four o'clock, Mike's father paged me to say that Evelyn would be delighted if I came. "We're both very grateful to you," he reiterated. I laughed to myself but agreed to come.

"Oh yes, I remember," Mike replied. "I felt

guilty about leaving early to visit Judith—my, uh, how shall I put it? Uh, my first love. You were gone by the time I got back."

By now my friends had drifted away, sensing that Mike and I were venturing into personal territory, perhaps miffed that I had not introduced them, and the two of us stood alone near the food table. Mike put a few crackers, a slice of brie, a couple of shrimp, and some grapes on his plate and reminisced. Between mouthfuls, he told me what I had never known. "Toward the end of my sophomore year in high school, my father gave me a pair of tickets a patient had given him to a concert at Carnegie Hall. With my heart in my mouth I invited Judith, one of the most beautiful and intelligent girls in my class. She didn't say 'no' outright; she said she'd have to ask her parents since the concert was on a school night. They gave permission and on the appointed evening I called for her and we took the BMT subway to the 57th Street station. I fell in love with Brahms' Fourth Symphony that night."

"With the symphony or with Judith?" I asked.

"With the symphony. I was already in love with Judith." He paused to pluck off a grape. "You know how much I love Brahms' Fourth. When I brought Judith home, I asked if she'd go out with me the following Saturday. Then the bomb dropped. She had a steady boyfriend, coming home from college that weekend. With a car no less. None of this subway stuff. I wasn't even old enough to have a learner's permit," Michael laughed. "I bought an LP of Brahms' Fourth with my allowance and took solace in listening to it—again and again. Drove my parents crazy."

"Sorry, Molly, this must be boring to you, but last night was the first I had heard about Judith. It cast a different light on Michael."

"No worries," Molly replied.

"If you were a man, I don't think I'd be telling you half of this."

Molly smiled and put her hand on mine. "Continue at your own pace. I know this must be hard for you."

Michael seemed to relish telling me the story, amusingly self-deprecating, but without concern for my sensibilities.

"Anyway, Judith and I never dated again," he said. "Then in my senior year, on the day you came to dinner, she called and said she was going to babysit for a cousin of hers who lived in the same apartment house as we did, and would I like to keep her company. When she called, I didn't know you were coming to dinner that evening—"

"If you had known," I interrupted, giving him a chance to redeem himself, "would you have canceled your visit with Judith?"

Up until this point, Mike had been looking at his plate, or at the people leaving the auditorium, or at the helpers. Now he glanced directly at me, wondering, I suppose, why this withered old lady had asked such a question. "Well, Judith was my first love, so—," he plucked another grape and chewed it thoughtfully. "So, I don't know," he answered, seemingly oblivious to our past relationship.

"It was just as well you left early to visit, uh, Judith," I murmured, only half intending Michael to hear. If he did, he showed no sign.

The reception lounge was almost empty and

the staff had started to clean up. I thought of sticking out my hand and saying "Goodbye, see you in another forty years." Instead I asked, "Where are you staying tonight?"

He pulled the plastic room key card from his pocket and held it at arm's length. "The Radisson."

"I guess you've rented a car?" Mike nodded. "Would you care to stop off at my house, have a drink, and catch up? The Radisson's not far from where I live." He hesitated. I don't know why I chose that moment to tell him about my late husband. "Donald died in an automobile accident two years ago. He skidded on a patch of ice coming down our driveway, lost control, and slammed into a tree. No air bags, and he didn't like seat belts."

Grasping my arm lightly, Mike said, "Oh, Joan, I am so sorry." He glanced at his watch. "I've got an eight o'clock flight tomorrow morning, so I should get back to the hotel soon." He slipped into his coat, hesitating. "OK, for old times' sake."

By the time we emerged from the lecture hall, the snow had tapered off and the plows had cleared the walkways and roads. A searing wind suggested more snow was on the way. When we reached Michael's car, I said, "Wait here. I'll drive my car over and you can follow me." A few minutes later I pulled up alongside him, flicked my lights, and drove slowly as Michael pulled out. Before long we were in the country. Around a curve in the road, my headlights caught the trees laced with snow. How evanescent, I thought sadly. By morning, the wind will have left nothing but skeletal branches.

"Tell me about the camp that you and Michael were

at," Molly interrupted. "Is that where you met?"
     "Yeah."

Camp Whitebirch, a boys' camp in the Berkshires. I had taken the job of camp doctor there to be near my mother. Dad had died suddenly the previous winter and mom would be spending the summer alone in our small family cottage across the lake from Whitebirch. When I told her about the job, she smiled delightedly then scoffed, "You know Joan, I can take care of myself. Our friends down the road are still there. Besides what will people think: a lady doctor at a boys' camp. You're not looking for a husband, are you?"

The idea had never occurred to me. In medical school, where I was one of only five women in my class, and in my pediatric residency, where I was one of two, I had to spend almost all my time around men. The one time I let myself be seduced I learned quickly he was only interested in sex and stopped the relationship. I made no effort to make myself appealing and cursed as roughly as my male colleagues. Many of them looked at me more as a competitor than a woman. My love was the kids I cared for.

Molly interrupted. "How well did you get to know him that summer at Whitebirch?"

Mike was a junior counselor, assisting in the care of seven-year-olds. The damp, moldy bunks triggered his asthma. More than once he came to my dispensary for a shot of adrenalin. When his parents visited in midsummer, they thanked me with a gift of an LP of Brahms' Fourth Symphony—maybe a new one, but maybe the one he had played over and over again to mourn the loss of his first love. Maybe his mother was tired of hearing it.

The snow was falling lightly as I reached the intersection at which I turned on to the road to the right. Michael dutifully followed.

"Even telling you now, Molly, I smile tenderly, recalling how we had joked around in that long-ago summer."

When one of his campers complained of a belly ache, Michael brought him to the dispensary and peered over my shoulder as I palpated his abdomen. "I think everything is OK," I told the camper, and his counselor.

"No, it's not," Michael observed, pointing to the boy's waist, where the indentations from the elastic band on his undershorts were plainly visible. "His underwear is too tight."

Playing along, I clapped my hand to my forehead. "How did I miss that?" I paused for dramatic effect, then turned to Michael, "Brilliant, Doctor! Have this boy go without underwear until the pain subsides. If the pain returns, we'll have to put him on a strict diet; no ice cream!" He got better quickly. Michael thought my imitation of Groucho Marx, especially his walk, was hilarious. Sometimes I embellished it by putting on a fake moustache.

"Is there more about, uh, Mike's asthma?" Molly asked.

"I'm coming to that."

A few weeks later, Mike came to the dispensary around ten in the evening. I was chatting with Ned, a good-looking counselor in his mid-twenties. Michael's shoulders were hunched as he gasped for air, his face gray and drawn, the wheeze audible when he exhaled. I took a vial of adrenalin from the refrigerator and drew up 0.3 cc while Mike rolled up his sleeve. Within minutes, he relaxed his shoulders and a boyish smile that could melt ice spread over his handsome face. "You saved my life, Doctor," he exclaimed melodramatically, and stooped to kiss my hand.

I put the vial back in the refrigerator and turned to Ned and Michael. "How would you boys like to listen to Brahms' Fourth Symphony?" I asked. "Michael's parents gave me the LP as a present." Ned was noncommittal but Mike, rolling his sleeve down, was eager. "I love Brahms' Fourth," he said.

The phonograph was in my room in the infirmary, a few steps from the dispensary; no campers were patients at the time, so we wouldn't be bothering anyone. The portable record player sat on my footlocker alongside my bed, its cord reaching up to a receptacle screwed into the bare socket that hung from the ceiling. With just one chair, the only place we could all sit was on my bed, one side of which was pushed against the rear wall. Ned stretched out on the side nearest the wall; while I took the LP from its jacket and placed it on the turntable, Mike lay down on his back next to Ned. I started the record and then lay down on my back next to Michael, not entirely on the bed. "Hey, you guys, I'm falling off the bed. Can't you scrunch up?" Ned groaned but turned on his side, facing out. Mike did likewise and I followed—a triple spoon, facing the phonograph.

As the second movement reached its denouement with a long, drawn-out, melancholy chord, a hand caressed my breast. It was not my habit to wear a bra after my evening swim. I became aroused. When the movement ended, none of us stirred. I put my hand over the one that cupped my breast. "Whose hand is this?" The hand squeezed gently, arousing me further.

"What are you talking about?" Ned replied.

Michael was silent. No one moved or spoke. Finally, I asked, "Should we play the other side?"

"I'm going to turn in," Ned replied. Michael and I swiveled off the bed so Ned could get out. "What about you, Mike?" Ned asked.

"It would be heresy to interrupt Brahms," Michael replied.

A flashing red traffic light interrupted my reverie. I put my left signal on and waited for Mike to stop behind me. He turned after me and I resumed my recollection.

The hall floor of the infirmary was cold on my bare feet as I returned to Michael after seeing Ned out and locking the door. I took the folded blanket from the foot of the bed and spread it over Mike, who was lying on his back, hands under his head. I turned the record over, gently placed the needle arm on the outer rim, and crawled under the blanket. I desperately wanted a cigarette but in deference to Mike's asthma postponed my smoke.

During the turbulent third movement, Michael whispered, "Don't you feel like you're perched perilously on the orbit of an electron?"

"Yes," I whispered back. "Did you just make

that up?"

Unromantically, he replied, "No, I plagiarized a poetic classmate."

"It's still apt," I answered. Turning to face Michael, I put my arm around him and whispered again, "Maybe I want to get knocked off."

As the French horns heralded the majestic finale, he turned to me and we drew closer. It was impossible to tell who initiated the kiss. By the time the symphony ended we were naked under the covers. I had not made love since that dead-end seduction in my residency and had almost forgotten how glorious it could be. The first time, Michael came quickly, oblivious to my unfulfilled desire. As he lay still afterwards, his head nuzzled in my neck, I asked, "Have you ever done this before?" He shook his head and I felt him getting aroused. His second time was better for me.

Almost home, my headlight caught the dark, round eyes of a young deer. I put the brakes on gently and it skittered over the snowbank.

After the symphony ended, the record must have spun for twenty minutes, making a click for every revolution, before I lifted the needle arm to its resting position. Michael dressed and after several deep kisses returned reluctantly to his sleeping seven-year-olds.

Propped up on my bed, I lit a cigarette. What had gotten into me? Was I titillated that an eighteen-year-old found me attractive, or that I would be the one to take away a boy's virginity? Impractically, was I in love with this kid? Was he in love with me, or had he just been waiting for the opportunity since pubescence? Now, forty years later, after hearing him go on about his "first love," I no longer had any illusion that Michael was in love with me back then. If I had any thoughts of rekindling a relationship, Michael going on about Judith had dashed them.

With four-wheel drive, my car had no trouble negotiating the driveway despite its incline. I parked in the garage, leaving space for Michael to turn around so he wouldn't have to back down on his way out. His rental car skidded once but he managed the wheel well and parked in front of the garage. The snow was starting to fall more heavily again, accumulating on the driveway.

I led Michael through the garage and into the grimy boot room. "Don't bother to take your shoes off, just give them a good wipe on the mat. Hang your coat over there." I pointed to a hook. Michael complied and followed me through the kitchen into the living room where I switched on two small lamps. While I built a fire, Michael wandered around the room, glancing at the masks and paintings, and at photos of places Donald and I had visited. When I stood, he was at the baby grand piano glancing at a photo of Donald in a faculty gown with multi-colored hood, a mortarboard in his hand.

"Your husband?"

"Yes, Donald. Good looking, don't you think?" I brushed the cinders off my hands. "What can I get you? You weren't old enough to drink the last time I saw you."

"You wouldn't happen to have single malt Islay Scotch?"

Molly jotted "Scotch" in a pad on her desk.

"I do. It was Donald's favorite on cold nights. With some water?" Michael nodded.

When I returned, Michael was looking at a watercolor on the wall behind the piano of an old woman working in her garden, bright sunlight highlighting her features.

"My mother," I volunteered. "I painted it."

"You are a woman of many talents." He pointed to the piano. "Do you still play?"

"A little, but arthritis is a hindrance." I handed Michael his Scotch and sat down next to him on the sofa. "Cheers." I clinked my wine glass against his tumbler. "Are you married?"

"Happily. My wife, Alice, is a partner at a big law firm where she specializes in sexual harassment cases. We have two children, fully grown. What about you?"

I pointed to the piano. Next to Donald's photos were pictures of our Chinese daughter and African son when they were eleven and fourteen. "Both married now, each with a kid of their own. I'm a grandmother!"

"How stupid of me," he exclaimed. "I should have connected them with the photo of your husband." He sipped his Scotch. "Are you still practicing pediatrics?"

"I've got to make a living. Donald left me his pension, but I'm trying to keep it in reserve. Taking care of children is what keeps me going."

We were silent for a moment, staring into the blazing fire, its heat not yet penetrating the chilly gloom. Restless, I got up to get my cigarettes and matches. As I struck the match I remembered. "Do you still have asthma?"

"Yeah, but it's under control with inhaled steroids—they weren't around forty years ago. Go ahead." He paused while I lit up. "I'm surprised you still smoke."

I took a deep drag and exhaled slowly. "It's the one vice I allow. I still take risks."

"I didn't know you were a risk-taker."

Now is as good a time as any, I thought. "Were you that naïve when we made love in the infirmary?" I lifted an ashtray from the piano and returned, this time to a soft leather chair opposite the sofa.

Michael winced. "That's an overused figure of speech," he replied, ignoring the thrust of my question.

"You mean, 'made love'?" I reached for my wine. "I suppose you're right. Love entails some commitment, and I didn't expect any from you and I'm sure you didn't expect any from me." I stood. "Shall I freshen up your Scotch?"

"I've got to be driving soon." He hesitated and then handed me his glass. "Just a smidgen."

When I returned with his drink, Michael was looking through the collection of LPs that Donald had organized in alphabetical order by composer. He pulled out one and held it up. "Your parents gave that to me for taking care of your asthma. I'm sure they never imagined you and I would—what shall I say?— fucked to Brahms' Fourth."

"You used to surprise me, Joan, with how crude you could be."

"You said 'make love' was an overused term, so I tried 'fucked.' That's what it was, wasn't it?" Michael took a long gulp but said nothing.

I lit another cigarette. "I liked you, Michael.

You were a sweet kid. Smarter than most, not too taken with yourself, funny, good around your campers." I chuckled. "Except for the time when you told them there was a whale in the lake and they all refused to go in the water." I took a puff. "Until you put your hand on my breast, I never dreamed of—sorry—making love with you."

"No," he laughed bitterly. "I crashed your private party with Ned." He peered through his glass at the crystalline ice, looking into the past, not the future. His next question came as if he had hurled his Scotch, ice and all, in my face. "How many others did you screw at camp that summer?"

I took a long drag. Finally, in as caustic a tone as I could muster, I replied, "You sound like your mother."

Mike sank back into the sofa. "I beg your pardon?"

Standing, I took another drag, picked up the ashtray, stamped out my cigarette, and circled around the room, Michael following me with his eyes. Stopping in front of him, I put down the ashtray and lit up again. "I've often wondered, Michael, what would have happened if you hadn't gone to visit, uh, Judith, the night I came to dinner. Until tonight, I didn't know how special Judith was to you." I inhaled deeply, slowly blowing the smoke out. "And I have to tell you that learning about her tonight hurt. You probably fantasized that you were making love to Judith in the infirmary instead of me." Without asking, I picked up his glass, empty now except for the ice, returned to the kitchen, and absent mindedly filled it with more Scotch than water.

Molly jotted a note.

He had taken off his sports coat and lain it on the sofa. He gratefully accepted the refill and took a swig. After another moment, he asked, "Why did you mutter at the reception that it was just as well I left? What did you and my parents talk about?"

"They didn't tell you anything?" A log crackled in the fireplace.

"No, they were asleep when I got home from my visit with Judith. I slept late the next morning. Dad was at work and mom was out shopping. It never came up after that. Maybe I was preoccupied, thinking about college, and Judith."

I sat down opposite Michael, took a sip of wine, and inhaled.

"When you left before dessert, your parents apologized. I said I didn't mind, trying to decide whether it was time to leave or tell them I had something on my mind. I reached in my bag for my car keys and came out with my cigarettes. Lucky Strikes. 'We don't smoke here,' your mother said severely. I dropped the pack back in my bag as we moved to the living room for coffee. After the niceties of sugar, cream, and stirring were completed, I said, 'There's something I should tell you.' They looked at me expectantly. I sipped my coffee. Finally, I announced, 'I'm pregnant.'"

"Oh my god!" Molly said.

Michael's jaw dropped, and he gasped. "What?"

"You heard me." Realizing the implication

instantly, he downed his third Scotch.

"Your mother congratulated me, not expecting the bomb that was about to explode. Your father was suspicious. 'Who's the father?' he asked. I told him it was you. Your mother jumped up. 'Michael's still a baby and would never do anything like that.' 'He's eighteen, dear,' your father said, still seated and remaining calm. 'That may be, but he knows better. I need a cigarette,' she replied. I reached in my bag and offered her a Lucky, and a light. After a few puffs, she asked, 'How did it happen?' 'We don't need the details, dear,' your father replied. 'I'll bet you seduced him, you bitch,' your mother said. 'I bet you've slept with all the unmarried counselors in camp, and maybe some married ones. How do you know Mike's the father?' I didn't expect compassion; maybe I should have expected the insults. I told your parents I hadn't made love—that was the term I used—for a very long time. Then it was your father's turn. 'Did you take precautions, Joan?' Fighting back tears after your mother's cruelty, I could only shake my head. 'Then why did you go all the way?' he asked. I tearfully told them I should have known better."

Michael got up, empty glass in hand, and stood facing the fire. His shadow loomed on the opposite wall. I took his empty glass, refilled it once more, and handed it to him, still facing the fire. He turned to me, accepted the drink, and took a swallow. "At freshman orientation after I arrived at college that fall," he began quietly, "we had a bull session in the men's dorm. My classmates boasted about their accomplishments— one, a violinist, had soloed with the Detroit Symphony; another had a novel published; a third had won the Westinghouse Science Talent prize—but none of them had gone 'all the way.' That was my claim to fame. They craved details. I didn't mention your name or where it happened, only that you were a doctor."

He turned, put his drink down, picked up a log and threw it on the fire. "My behavior in that bull session has bothered me ever since. One of the boys asked if I had used a condom. 'Weren't you worried about getting her pregnant?' he asked. 'Remember,' I answered, 'she's a doctor. She knows how to manage these things.'" Michael sat back down on the sofa, opposite me. "These things," he repeated, turning again to the fire. The only sounds were the hiss and crackle of the logs. "I thought then that doctors had a lot more capability than I now know to be the case."

The log Michael had thrown on the fire flared. "Shall I continue?" I asked. He nodded. "Your mother stood in front of me, pointed to the door, and said, 'Get out of my apartment, you whore,' angrily ignoring what I had just said. I gathered my bag and got up, but your father sat me down. 'The pregnancy is a lot worse for Joan than it is for Michael,' he said to your mother. He turned to me and asked, 'Do you want the baby?' Calmed by his rational line of questioning, I told your parents that I didn't see how I could have it, or keep it if I had to have it. 'Do you and Michael love each other?' your father asked me."

"Ah, zat word again," Michael slurred with a sinister sigh.

"I told them I was fond of you; you were smart, amusing, and tender. I told you you had never said you loved me, and I had never said I loved you, and I reminded them I was eleven years older than you. I said, 'I'd ruin Michael's life if we married and had the baby.' Your father asked me if I had considered an abortion. I had, of course, but who would do it? That was before *Roe v. Wade*. He said he could arrange one if I could get a few days off. 'Of course, we'll pay for it,' he added. I still can't believe what your mother said next: 'How can we afford to when we haven't paid off the Cadillac?'"

"So, you had the abortion?" Michael finished his latest Scotch.

"It didn't go well. It was done in a doctor's office in Brooklyn. I bled profusely and ended up with a hysterectomy."

Michael looked incredulous. He turned to look at the pictures of my kids on the piano. "Well, at least you have kids, Joan."

At that moment, I could have killed him. I love my son and daughter dearly, but the guilt of what I had done, the pain of the abortion, the bleeding, the hysterectomy, the sterility—all for Michael. I lit another cigarette. "That's true," I said flatly. "After my fellowship, I moved up here, went into practice with another pediatrician, met and married Donald, adopted our kids, and buried the past."

Now that I had finished telling Michael the story, I wished he would leave.

"Didja tell Donald?" he asked.

"I didn't use your name—it would have meant nothing to him—but yes, I had to tell him why I couldn't have children." Picking the glass up by its stem, I finished my wine.

Michael struggled to his feet. "Really must be goin'," he slurred. I helped him on with his sports jacket. On his way to the boot room he swayed uncontrollably.

Molly looked at Joan, surprised at her awareness of Michael's intoxication. She thought of Miranda rights but said nothing.

Fetching his coat, I told him, "Turn left out of the driveway and keep going straight. You'll see the Radisson in half a mile on your left." I opened the garage door to let him out. A few inches of snow had fallen. He stumbled as he took his car keys out but caught himself on the car's door handle. I waved weakly as he started the car, closed the garage door, and opened the door to the boot room.

"Did you go straight to bed?" Molly asked.

I emptied the ashtray, washed out the glasses, and put the dark green bottle of Scotch back in the kitchen cabinet, surprised to see it was almost empty. I made sure the front door was locked, picked up the LP of Brahms' Fourth, and dropped the record on the turntable, not noticing which side was up. The third movement startled me with its ebullient fortissimo. What was it Michael had said when we lay next to each other forty years ago? "Perched perilously on the orbit of an electron." I had been knocked off! "Knocked off and knocked up," I remember saying out loud.

While the fourth movement played, I got ready for bed, then came down to the living room, switched off the stereo, and put Brahms' Fourth away.

I fell asleep quickly and had a dream. Michael and I were making love in the infirmary. We approached climax leisurely, each attuned to the other's wants. Then I heard knocking. "Come back later," I yelled. Still the knocking. Louder. I awoke.

Someone was knocking on the front door. The LED clock on the night table said 6:20. It was still dark.

I put on my robe, walked downstairs, turned the porch light on, and peered out at a state trooper. "Sorry to bother you so early, Doctor. Do you know a Michael Silver?"

"Yes." In the frigid air, I clutched the robe's lapels around my throat.

"You'll be cold standing here. Do you mind if I come in?" I opened the door wide and let him into the vestibule. "It might be best if we sit down." I showed him into the kitchen, and we sat opposite each other at the table. "At about midnight last night, Professor Silver seems to have lost control of his car, swerved into the ongoing lane, and struck a pickup truck head on."

"Oh my god!"

"The pickup's driver was killed instantly. Professor Silver is in the county hospital, comatose, with multiple injuries. He would have died instantly were it not for the seat belt." He paused, waiting perhaps for another reaction from me. I remained silent. "We found an invitation to the Hooper lecture in his jacket pocket, saying that he was the lecturer. We notified the dean, who told us that you were one of the people who had been talking to Professor Silver after the lecture. We're contacting each of them."

"Yes, I had asked him a question and he gave me a long answer." Stunned with the news, I asked, "Have you notified Professor Silver's wife?"

"Yes, she's on her way here now. Do you know her?" I shook my head.

At that moment, the trooper's walkie-talkie announced that he was to proceed immediately to the site of another accident; the snowstorm was wreaking havoc. I walked him back to the front door. He turned as he left, "If you know more about Professor Silver's whereabouts last night, please get in touch with us." He handed me a card with the contact information for the state police.

Dressing quickly, I brewed a cup of coffee. Why had I not told the trooper that I was probably the last person to see Michael before the accident? My office hours for infants and toddlers—I did not see school-age children until after school, except for emergencies—started at nine. I resolved to go to the state police headquarters after my morning hours. I had never been there before.

*

Detective Michell had let Joan talk, almost without interruption. When she finally finished, Molly sat back in her chair, gazing at the ceiling for almost a minute. Then she looked down at the pad on which she had taken notes and asked, "Dr. Greenfield, when you told Professor Silver about your hysterectomy, you said, 'At that moment, I could have killed him.'"

"Did I?"

"Were you still that angry when he left?"

"I was angry. I wanted him out of my house. I probably wasn't very hospitable. Did I wish him dead?—No."

"You also said that the bottle of Scotch was almost empty when you put it back in the cabinet." I nodded. "How full was it when you poured his first drink?"

"Oh, I guess more than half."

"And you were drinking wine?"

"Only a glass or two."

"How long would you say he was in your house?"

"We must have arrived around nine-thirty. I turned my light out just before midnight. About two hours."

Again, Molly was silent for almost a minute. "You know, Dr. Greenfield, in some states a host who allows a guest to drink to the point of intoxication may be held liable for an injury incurred as a result of his drinking. This state happens not to be one of them." She stood. "Thank you for being so candid, Dr. Greenfield. If you are planning to leave town in the next few weeks, please let us know where we can reach you." She opened the door, shook hands, and showed Joan out.

Only a Game

On Fridays, the dominant conversation around the oval conference table was the previous night's episode of *Survivor*. From senior faculty to dishwasher, some with brown bags, others with plastic trays from the cafeteria, they had a communal lunch in the seminar room. Some lamented the elimination of a favorite from the reality show; others were glad that so-and-so was still in the running. Content to chew on his sandwich and an overripe pear, Victor, a professor of molecular biology, enjoyed seeing them so animated. But the source of their animation bothered him. He didn't own a television and had never watched *Survivor*.

"What do you find so appealing about this program?" Victor asked Ann one Friday after lunch as they walked down the broad corridor to their adjacent labs. She was an assistant professor in her mid-thirties, with two small kids who were enrolled in the university's day-care program and a husband on the faculty in mathematics. Victor couldn't imagine how she found time to watch television, yet from her active participation in the lunch-time conversation, he knew she watched *Survivor*.

"I guess because it's not scripted; nobody knows the winner until the contest is over."

"But there must be a lot of pre-selection by the producers; it's not like a sample of the population picked at random?"

"No, I suppose not. Still, it's nice to know that real people can do this stuff. It's not exactly vicarious but I can identify with the contestants—at least some of them— knowing they're not actors." They reached the double doors that separated the labs from the administrative offices and conference rooms, each pushing open the door immediately ahead.

"From what I heard at lunch—and even from the title—*Survivor* seems highly competitive."

"Highly," Ann agreed, "but sometimes contestants form alliances."

"Still, the premise is one winner," said Victor, "the rest are losers. Fostering cooperation—I guess that's not high on the agenda."

They arrived at her lab. "I never thought of it that way," Ann replied. She opened the door to her lab, smiling at Victor. "Have a nice weekend," she said, disappearing into her lab.

Victor admired Ann, a young, attractive, intelligent woman, yet he was put off by her enjoyment of a genre in which there was one winner and many losers. *Why can't people be entertained by watching others work together so they could all be winners?* he asked himself. Throughout his career, he had gladly shared material and data from his own experiments, believing that cooperation was most likely to advance science. As it became evident that sequencing the human genome was a race to be won, he'd noticed that the amount of sharing had declined.

Instead of returning to his lab bench, where he was

working on a gene-sequencing experiment, he walked into his adjoining office. *What would people do if they had to choose between competition and cooperation to maximize their chance of survival?* he asked himself. *If I can find the right situation, I'll construct a game and try it out at lunch on Monday. Stranding the players in a wilderness is too much like Survivor, but coping with an impending disaster might be an alternative. But what kind of disaster?* He rejected a giant meteor approaching earth because individuals could not do much to stop it. A foreign military invasion seemed improbable in the United States, therefore, not suited for the American players of his game. He could make the players hostages captured by terrorists, in which the choice would be between individual escape and acting collectively to destabilize the captors. *But that is all too real and might disturb the players.* Finally, a different kind of disaster occurred to him—one that would pose a choice between cooperative and competitive action with less chance of upsetting anyone.

Instead of working on the gene-sequencing experiment, Victor started to draft a scenario and brought his laptop home over the weekend to work on it. On Monday morning, he printed eight copies of the final version, enough for everyone. Five people showed up for lunch and he distributed the handouts to them, explaining that it was a game he had devised, and assuring them it was not an intelligence test and there were no right or wrong answers. This is what he handed out:

> You live or work on an island that is connected to the mainland by a causeway. One day when you're on the island, a friend at the National Oceanic and Atmospheric Administration calls to say that the West Coast/Alaska Tsunami Warning Center has detected seismic activity of the type that precedes

a magnitude 7 earthquake under the Pacific. If the earthquake were to occur, the epicenter would be close enough for a tsunami to inundate the island within twelve hours. The scientists are still debating whether to issue a warning. Knowing you are on the island, your friend wanted to tell you what was happening. He cannot notify the other one thousand families and five hundred day workers who inhabit it. Most people who live there commute by car to work on the mainland; many of those who work on the island use public buses to travel from, and back to, the mainland.

Circle the ONE choice that indicates what you would do first. DO NOT SIGN YOUR NAME. Tear the paper along the dashed lines to separate your answer.

----

1. Do nothing; wait for official notification.
2. Leave the island at once.
3. Phone your neighbors, share the warning, and discuss what to do.

They all agreed to play, reading the scenario while they ate lunch and then circling their first choice.

With scissors supplied by Victor, they cut their handouts along the dashed lines, depositing the strips in a beaker Victor had brought from his lab. He handed it to Patrick, who was sitting immediately to his left, and asked him to read the choices while Victor got up to record them on the room's whiteboard. A gangly but not unhandsome postdoc in Victor's lab, Patrick had long, dirty blonde hair tied in a ponytail, and two-day stubble on his cheeks; he was wearing sandals, cut-offs, and a T-shirt with the name of a rock band on the front. At the whiteboard, Victor wrote the options with a green magic marker and entered the results as Patrick read them:

	Result
1. Do nothing; wait for official notification	1 (+ Joan)
2. Leave the island at once.	2
3. Phone your neighbors, share the warning, and discuss what to do.	1(+ Victor)

"One slip is blank," Patrick told Victor.

There was a moment of silence as all but one wondered who had reneged on their commitment to play the game. Finally, Joan, the labs' dishwasher and the only African American in the room, raised her hand and said timidly, "I guess that's me." They all looked at her. "Pardon me, Professor Victor, but no one from the National Oceanic whatever would call a black dishwasher to give her secret information."

Victor felt warm under his collar and blushed. "Yes, I suppose that's true, Joan. Forgive me, I should have worded it differently." He paused for a moment. "But let's say that you have the information. What would be your choice?"

Joan smiled diffidently. "I wouldn't have much of a choice; I couldn't leave the island at once 'cause I don't have a car and the buses us hired folks use usually run only at the beginning and the end of the workday. If there was one in the middle of the day and I left early to catch it, I'd be fired on the spot. Jobs are hard to come by. And so far as calling the neighbors: If I was a maid working on the island, I wouldn't have permission to use the phone, and if I did, who would listen to me anyway? Much as I would like to get off that island, I'd have to wait for official information."

"Thank you." Victor marked her answer accordingly. "Would anybody else like to tell us how they voted?"

Emboldened that his vote was not the only one for leaving, Patrick commented, "Waiting for official notification might be too late. I'd leave right away. If the tsunami never came, I'd lose the rest of the day on the island; I'd probably just have spent it loafing on the beach."

Emily, a petite pre-doc in Victor's lab with curly brown hair and owlish eyeglasses, giggled. "I'm the one who voted to tell the neighbors." She had a crush on Patrick but doubted he would ever pay attention to her. He had never spoken to her outside the lab, and inside it was always work-related and perfunctory. She launched a frontal assault. "You're thinking only of yourself, Patrick. You're taking advantage of personally knowing an expert. You're not thinking about the others who don't have your information and will be left behind." Surprised by the accusation, Patrick looked at her across the table. She stopped, returned Patrick's glance, and then looked down at the table. "That's why I would phone the neighbors, especially if I had nothing better to do than lie on the beach all day."

Emily had exposed Patrick's lazy, selfish streak. From her work in the lab, he knew she was smart, and though she hid behind her big glasses, she obviously was not shy, and not bad looking either. Nevertheless, he did not offer to change his vote.

"Suppose I called my neighbors," Ann, the assistant professor, spoke up, "and they all called their friends and there was a mass exodus and then nothing happened. I would look foolish, like the little boy who cried 'wolf.'" She smiled at Joan. "I'd wait for official notification, like Joan."

"My first reaction was to choose 'phone your neighbors,'" said another junior faculty member, "but if time was of the essence then I wouldn't be able to reach more than a handful. They in turn would have to take my word that the threat was real and imminent, which I couldn't be certain it was, and they would then have to pass on the message to others, with the same assurance I had conveyed to them, and so on down the line. It seems quite likely the message would get garbled along the way. In the meantime, valuable time would be wasted. I concluded that phoning would spread confusion and be no better than just leaving, which, reluctantly, is what I voted for." Patrick nodded, glad that his choice had been vindicated.

Ann turned to Victor. "We know this is your game, Victor, but you didn't vote."

"That's true," Victor replied. "I guess I should, now that you have all explained your votes." He moved his lunch bag aside. "Based on the discussions about *Survivor* around this table, I wanted to test the hypothesis that in life-threatening situations, people act competitively rather than cooperatively. The sample size is too small to draw any conclusions, especially since my vote—for telling my neighbors—makes it a three-way tie."

With that, people started to tidy up their lunch bags and leave.

When Emily, who had stayed to ask Victor a quick question about an experiment, left the conference room, she was surprised to find Patrick waiting in the corridor. "Hi," he smiled. "You made some good points, Emily." Patrick thought she was scowling at him. "Having to choose on the spur of the moment, I thought of myself."

If Emily was scowling, Patrick's last sentence turned it into a smile. "Thank you, Patrick. My first reaction was to get off the island as fast I could, too, but I

changed my mind when I realized how selfish that was."
They walked side by side back to the lab. By the time they
reached it, Emily had agreed to go to a movie with Patrick
that weekend. They went out together a few more times in
the ensuing two weeks. Living in separate cramped
apartments, each shared with several others, their physical
contact was limited to making out comfortably in Patrick's
second-hand, two-door Corolla.

On the third Monday after Victor's little game,
Emily told Patrick that her grandparents had announced
over the weekend that they were going to Europe for the
summer. "Grandma said I could use their house on
weekends while they're gone. It's on an island just off the
coast."

Patrick looked at her. "So?"

"Grandma thought it would be a good place to
study for my comps. She said I could bring a friend as long
as we left the house as we found it." Emily paused and
smiled. "She didn't say anything about the friend's gender."

Patrick caught on. "How far away is it?"

"About a two-hour drive, maybe a hundred miles,
connected to the mainland by a causeway."

"Are you inviting me?"

Emily grabbed Patrick's hand. "It's a beautiful
place; I spent parts of every summer there when I was a
kid. Body surfing, swimming, volleyball on the beach." She
paused, thinking about Victor's game, which had, after all,
sparked their relationship. "You can even lie on the beach
all day," she said, quickly adding, "with me, of course."

"I didn't think you thought much of lying on the
beach," he rejoindered.

"Not literally all day. There are other activities,
including study."

"No tsunamis?" he asked with a smile.

"Not that I ever heard of. They're rare along this coast." She did not mention that Tsunami hazard signs were placed at regular intervals along the beach.

At the appointed hour on a Saturday morning in late June, Patrick called for Emily in his second-hand Corolla. On the way out to the island, they tuned the radio to rock music and talked about their work in the lab and some of their mutual acquaintances, including Victor, their faculty adviser, whom they both liked but thought a bit old fashioned.

Just before they reached the causeway, Emily directed Patrick to stop at a small supermarket for provisions. With the Saturday influx, traffic moved slowly along the causeway, even though the traffic lights had been switched to favor new arrivals.

They parked in front of her grandparents' house, and Emily took Patrick's hand and walked him around the outside. "I've only dreamed of a house like this, right on the beach," Patrick told her. Under a cloudless sky, they glided arm in arm toward the gently rolling ocean lapping at the sand a short distance away. The concave beach curved for almost half a mile. Houses like the one belonging to Emily's grandparents dotted the shore at irregular intervals. "Looks like the tide is out," Emily observed.

They returned to the house and Emily unlocked the door, breathing in the familiar, not unpleasant musty smell of a seaside house that had been closed for a while. They fetched their backpacks and the provisions from the car. Patrick helped her open the windows on the first floor. Emily led him up the stairs, past the second floor where the master bedroom, her grandfather's study, and a guest room were located, to a third floor consisting only of her bedroom, unchanged since her childhood, and a small bathroom. She threw open the dormer window that faced the ocean and inhaled the sea breeze. Patrick came up behind her and took in the panoramic view. To the far left, she pointed out the tall masts rising above the beach, their hulls obscured by a clump of trees. "That's the island's marina," she explained. "There's a bar and a restaurant down there but not much night life."

Maintaining a show of decorum, Emily directed Patrick to put on his swimming trunks in her bedroom while she changed into a bikini in the bathroom. Admiring her figure in the mirror behind the bathroom door, Emily was aware of her heart pounding. She was pleased how she had cleverly turned her initial attack on Patrick—his selfish insistence on fleeing the island without warning others— into a mini love affair. *How far will Patrick want to go?* she wondered. *How far do I want to go?* She left her glasses alongside the sink.

Barefoot, they returned to the beach where Emily darted quickly into the surf. Fully immersed in the cool water, she splashed Patrick, prompting him to dive beneath the surface. They swam out about twenty-five yards and then turned and swam another fifty yards parallel to the beach. Emily returned to the shore first, yelling over her shoulder, "Race you to that sign there." She pointed down the beach and started to run on the firm, dark brown sand along the water's edge.

"What would Victor say if he knew you were so competitive?" Patrick asked as he caught up to Emily just before the sign.

"It's been bred into me since I was a kid, racing along this beach since I was old enough to run."

The sign was higher up on the beach, its message facing inland, away from the water. "Let's see what the sign says," Patrick suggested.

"Nothing interesting," Emily replied and turned to run back. But Patrick had started to trudge through the looser, lighter colored sand toward the sign. Reluctantly, she followed him. He reached the sign and turned to read it. "TSUNAMI HAZARD ZONE," Patrick said out loud. Below was a silhouette of a giant wave and a person running away from it. He turned to Emily, "Why didn't you tell me?"

"Well, we've never had one along this coast." She took Patrick by the hand to lead him toward the house.

"There's always a first time," he said, a tinge of anxiety in his voice.

"They'd warn us, like in Victor's little game."

"But that might be too late. Like I said Emily, I'd get out as quickly as I could." They walked silently along the water's edge, where the sand was moist and cool.

"Aren't you hungry? All that exercise worked up my appetite," Emily said as they neared the house.

Patrick made a tuna fish salad from the provisions they had purchased. Emily cut some salami and Monterey Jack into small cubes and opened a box of Triscuit. They brought their lunch out to the wooden deck at the back of the house. Emily went back inside and returned with two bottles of beer from the refrigerator.

After lunch they lay side by side in a spacious hemp hammock that occupied part of the deck, made unintrusive love, read insubstantial paperbacks, fell asleep, and went for another swim. They went to the restaurant near the marina for dinner, returning home around eight-thirty, slightly drunk on a bottle of Pinot Grigio. *At last the birth control pills are about to pay off,* Emily thought. They undressed each other in the living room, lit only by fading daylight, lay on the carpeted floor, and leisurely approached climax as darkness set in.

The rotating red light of a police car, thrown intermittently on the walls of the living room, followed shortly by a knock on the door, interrupted them. "Oh shit," Emily whispered guiltily, "they've caught us."

"What do you mean 'caught us'? What have we done?" Ignoring the question, she raced up to her room and returned wearing an old terry beach robe cinched around her waist. She shooed Patrick into the kitchen, found her glasses on the floor, and smoothed her hair as she walked to the door.

"Sorry to bother you, Ma'am," the uniformed policeman said. Emily had never been called that before. "We saw a strange car in the driveway and thought someone might be breaking in. The house was dark."

"It's my friend's. My grandma's letting us use the house for the weekend. Everything's fine here," she replied in a childlike voice.

"I'm afraid it's not. We've received a tsunami warning." Emily clutched the robe to her throat. "You're probably too far out to have heard the siren. We've been asked to tell people to evacuate the island."

"Now? We just got here a few hours ago." Standing at the open door, she noticed a few cars, their headlights on, heading toward the causeway.

"I'd suggest you stop what you're doing and leave immediately." He hesitated. "It's not a sure thing and I can't order you to leave, but it certainly is better to be safe than sorry."

"What about the house?" Emily asked anxiously.

"There's not much you can do. Close all the windows, move valuables to the top floor, and hope for the best." The policeman looked at his watch. "Sorry, Miss, I've got others to warn. Good luck."

Emily closed the door and stood in the dark

hallway. *If I tell Patrick, he'll want to leave. Is that what I want?*

Patrick was standing in front of the refrigerator, the only light in the room, when Emily entered. He took out the quart of milk they had bought. "Do you want some?" he asked Emily.

"Half a glass," she mumbled as if in a daze. They sat at the kitchen table. Patrick broke the silence. "What did the cop want?"

Emily seemed lost in thought. "What?"

"What did the cop want?" he repeated.

"Oh!" She seemed to revive. "Nothing much. He saw an unfamiliar car in the driveway and wanted to make sure it wasn't burglars." She got up; her robe fell open as she threw her arms around Patrick. "Let's go up to my room." Patrick gulped his milk and followed obediently. This time their love making was not interrupted. Finally content, they fell asleep.

It was barely light when Emily got out of bed. The temperature had dropped, and she put on the chemise she had brought and walked two steps to the open dormer window. The cool air felt good on her body, but something seemed strange. It was totally quiet; the surf was not lapping at the shore. It took a minute for her eyes to grow accustomed to the early dawn light and she could not see out to the water's edge. She retrieved her glasses but still could not see the water. She looked to the left, beyond the point of the beach. There were no masts bobbing in the pale light. Beyond where the masts should have been, she saw a dim outline of a mountain she had never noticed before. At first, she thought it was because she had never looked in that direction, but as she watched the mountain grew higher and closer, traveling obliquely toward their crescent beach. She turned to Patrick for an instant; he was still asleep. Fascinated, she stared at the oncoming mass. In back of her, the sun appeared above the horizon, illuminating the curl in front of the crest in which the boats, yanked from their moorings, tumbled like toys, their masts and hulls shattered. A roar like a jet flying close to land broke the silence as the wave loomed over her. Emily ran back to her bed and threw herself on top of Patrick.

*

The sun shining through the dormer window awakened Patrick. He was surprised to find Emily, still asleep, clinging to him in her nightshirt, which was soaked with sweat. Disentangling from her, he grabbed his pants and went quietly to the bathroom. When he returned a few minutes later, she was sitting up in bed, weeping. As he approached, she gasped, "You're alive!"

"She pulled him back to bed and hugged him.

"Your night shirt is soaked, Emily. You must have had a bad dream."

Slowly, she was able to control her breathing. "It was so real." She told him how she had gotten out of bed before sunrise, gone to the dormer window and seen that the water had run out way past the low tide mark. "That's what happens in a tsunami." Her knowledge surprised him. "Wait, do me a favor, Patrick. Go to the window and look toward the marina." He did as he was told. "What do you see?"

"Tall masts bobbing beyond the clump of trees. Just like yesterday."

She shook her head in disbelief. "Lemme ask you one question: Last night, did a policeman come to the door?"

"Are you wondering whether that was part of your dream?" She nodded weakly. "Yes, Emily, you told me he wanted to know what my car was doing in front of your house."

"Oh, Patrick, I did something terrible." She gasped again. "I lied to you."

"He wasn't a cop?"

Emily started to cry again. Patrick sat on the edge of the bed, not touching her.

"He was a cop all right and he did want to know about your car. But he told me something else." She paused, checking to make sure she would not erupt into tears again. "He came to tell me there was a tsunami warning. 'Stop what you're doing and leave immediately,' he said."

"Why didn't you tell me?"

She burst into tears again and reached for his hand, but he withdrew it. "I didn't want to stop what we were doing," she sobbed.

Patrick made no effort to comfort her. "Do you think the danger has passed?" Exasperated, he exclaimed, "Oh, how would you know?" He went down to the kitchen where he remembered seeing a list of telephone numbers on the refrigerator door. He found one for the local police department and punched the number into his cell phone. "About the tsunami. Is the coast clear?" He listened intently. "Thank you very much."

Briskly, he walked up the two flights of stairs. "Pack your stuff. We're leaving."

"What did you learn?"

"There's been no tidal wave yet. The warning's gone from code red to code orange."

"It's been more than twelve hours since the policeman came by," Emily said rationally. "By now the wave must have dissipated or made landfall someplace else."

"Look, Emily, I'm leaving," he replied angrily. "If you want to stay on the island, you'll have to stay by yourself; you can take the bus back to the mainland."

The thought horrified her. She had never taken the bus before and didn't know the schedule, or even where the nearest bus stop was.

Reluctantly, she tossed her few belongings into her backpack, including her damp bikini and chemise. Downstairs, she packed the unused food and drink they'd bought into the plastic bags they came in. Driving to the causeway, they joined several other cars leaving the island. "You see, we're not the only ones left," Emily said.

He did not answer and they did not speak another word on the entire trip. They didn't even turn on the car radio. At her apartment, Emily got out silently and slammed the car door shut. She took a step and then quickly turned back before he pulled away. "I forgot my backpack." She reached in to pull it out. "You can keep the food." She slammed the door again.

*

Over lunch the following Monday, Victor, Patrick, and four others discussed the tsunami that had struck the coast late the previous day. Emily was not there. The news reported that the lower floors of beachfront houses hit by the wave had flooded, but there was no loss of life and all persons were accounted for. Patrick told them a friend had invited him to spend the weekend on an island off the coast which had, according to the news, sustained damage. "The police went door to door to warn people," he told his lunchmates, "but how could they know every person who was on the island?"

"What did you do when you got the warning?" several of them asked at once.

"Like I said in Victor's game last month, I left as soon as I heard." He recalled Emily's last remark. "But others stayed."

"That's incredible," Victor said sharply. "They could have lost their lives by not fleeing."

"It doesn't surprise me," Ann argued. "It's not like a wildfire, where people can smell the smoke, maybe even see the flames advancing."

Patrick wondered how Emily would have defended herself if she had been at the lunch. He blushed as he recalled her explain, *I didn't want to stop what we were doing.* He didn't say anything.

Victor let out an audible sigh as he folded his lunch bag. "No more social experiments for me," he said to no one in particular. "Real life is more complex than any game; too many uncontrollable variables. I'll stick to the hard sciences."

Last Days of Summer

Set back thirty feet from the shore of Lake Clear, the cottage had been in Sarah's family for three generations. Built in the 1920s, it was a two-bedroom wood frame, with a stone fireplace in the central room providing heat on chilly summer days. In the 1950s, Sarah's parents had installed baseboard heating, and she and Noah had added a bunk room in 2000 to accommodate their grandchildren—the fourth generation. The cottage had inside plumbing, but because of the extreme cold of the Adirondack winters, the pipes, which were not buried deeply, had to be drained before frost, making it uninhabitable from November to April. No generation had installed a television, and even in 2016 the connection to the Internet was through a slow, sporadic, dial-up modem. Aside from the *Adirondack Daily Enterprise*, news was received from North Country Public Radio. But news was something to escape from, especially when the grandchildren were present; something to be left in the city, to be faced only on return from vacation. Neither Sarah nor Noah nor many others knew it at the time, but news that summer, when the campaigns for the presidency began in earnest after the party conventions, marked the beginning of a new era.

Sarah, who still stood straight as an arrow, came up to Noah's chin when they married, but now he was bent with age and she came up to his forehead. Although her face was etched with lines and her hair had turned silvery white, she had a sparkle in her blue eyes and spoke with wit and charm. In their early eighties, children of the Great Depression, they had been lifelong Democrats. For the first time, in 2016, they had disagreed on who the Democratic nominee should be. Sarah, thinking the time for a woman president was long overdue, staunchly supported Hillary Clinton. Noah had nothing against a woman president, but Bernie Sanders' outsider approach, refusing to take money from corporations and coming out strongly in favor of holding big banks accountable and reducing inequality, seemed at last to be returning the party to the direction it had taken under FDR (for whom he had been too young to vote) and his New Deal. They agreed that Trump would be a disaster; much worse than Reagan and the Bushes.

Sarah had enjoyed summers at the cottage since childhood. She introduced Noah to it when they were courting and made it a home away from home for their children and then their grandchildren. The cottage was the base for swimming, sailing, tennis, climbing the High

Peaks, and savoring soft ice cream at Donnelly's. But now the lake felt too cold for Sarah and Noah to enjoy beyond the briefest of dips on hot days. With the exception of the ice cream, which they consumed in moderation, they were too old for the other activities. The couple still walked together on paths along the lakes, but Sarah had not climbed since she had slipped on a rocky slab and broken her arm three years ago. Noah limited his hikes to short, less strenuous ones, like St. Regis and Ampersand mountains.

Their three children assumed more and more responsibility when they and their children visited—cooking, cleaning, keeping the place in good repair, organizing the activities. After they departed, Sarah resumed cooking and cleaning, which left her exhausted and lonely. She had broached with Noah the idea that the children should take over maintenance of the cottage; they were well enough off to afford the caretaker and repairs, and their jobs enabled them to take summer vacations of at least two weeks. By not coming all at once, they could keep the cottage occupied most of the summer. Sarah and Noah would visit as guests.

Noah resisted. Though shorter than he once was, and not as steady on his feet, he insisted he was still strong, even when she pointed out that he got out of breath more easily and walked more slowly than he used to. "Only to let you keep up," he snarled in response. Truth be told, except for steep grades on which she had always been more cautious, Sarah outwalked him.

By mid-September, after a lot of

discussion among themselves and with their children, Noah had begrudgingly agreed this would be their last summer as the primary owners. By the fourth Sunday, they had moved their clothing from the largest bedroom to what had been the guest bedroom and completed most of the end-of-season chores. They planned to return to the city the next day. Noah, awakening from his customary after-lunch nap, announced, "I think I'll climb Ampersand this afternoon."

"You're kidding," Sarah said, obviously miffed. She knew she had to marshal her arguments to dissuade him. "The weather report says possible rain tonight, with a chance of snow at the higher elevations."

Already putting on his hiking boots, Noah laughed. "I'll be back long before dark. Last time I got to the top in an hour and twenty minutes and down in less than an hour."

"You're five years older now," she reminded him. "Pick a turn-around time and stick to it."

"Sure," he said unconvincingly.

Conceding that she was going to lose this particular argument, Sarah said, "At least take your trekking poles."

"Good idea," he conceded. "Have you seen them?" She shook her head and he went to look for them. Immediately, she went into the kitchen, quickly made two peanut butter and jelly sandwiches, wrapped them, and put them in his backpack along with his Polartec jacket, headlamp, and a filled plastic water bottle. She was just finishing when he returned from the car.

"They were in the trunk all along. You must have put them there." She rolled her eyes at his accusation.

"Okay, Sarah, I'm off. See you by six."

"Aren't you forgetting something?" She held out his backpack.

"I was about to get it." He slung it over his shoulder. "Did you put rocks in it?"

"Just some light nourishment in case you happen to get delayed." He dropped the pack in the trunk. She came out to see him off. "Be careful," she said sincerely and kissed his lips.

"There'll be plenty of people on the mountain. If I get in trouble, somebody will help."

"Fine," she muttered. "Ruin their day as well as mine." She went back inside to finish packing.

*

Only one battered Ford pickup truck, with local plates and a Trump sticker on the rear bumper, was parked in the lot when Noah arrived at the trailhead. Two weeks ago, the lot could not hold all the cars—some with canoes or kayaks strapped to their roofs—which overflowed to the shoulders of the highway. Now, three days into autumn, people were thinking less about climbing mountains and more about school, jobs, and hunting. He left space for another car between the Ford pickup and his Camry, which sported a *Bernie 2016* sticker that he had refused to remove after Clinton won the nomination.

Noah popped the trunk, got out, stretched, and retrieved his trekking poles and day pack. He walked behind the pickup on his way to the trail. *I didn't think Trump people climbed mountains*, he said to himself. The weather was perfect: high cumulus clouds scattered in a sea of blue, an occasional rustle in the air, yellow swatches and red blushes among the evergreens.

It was three o'clock when he crossed the road to the trailhead, surprised at the length of his shadow. He signed the trail register with the pencil stub in the box and wrote "1" in the column for "Number of people in party." No one else had signed for that date; *Trump people would never check in—smacks of regulation,* he grumbled to himself. The trail started on a long level stretch, over wooden planks in swampy areas. On such terrain his poles were more nuisance than help. The forest still showed signs of lumbering a hundred years earlier: spruce and pine that had not yet attained their full height; beech, birch, maple—all competing for the sunlight that dappled the forest floor. Noah looked at his watch when he reached what was left of the clearing. It was three-forty. *I used to make it in under thirty minutes.* Years ago, when a fire tower stood atop the mountain, the clearing was the site of a ranger's cabin. Now both the tower and cabin were gone and the forest had closed in. He moved on quickly, beginning the steep ascent that would continue with only short interruptions to the top. *If I get to the summit by five, I'll be lucky.* At a point where the trail turned abruptly, a short spur led to an open ledge. Walking to its edge, Noah looked north to Saranac Lake below. The mountain's shadow had already spread over its western shore. He unscrewed his water bottle and took a sip. Although warm from his uphill exertion, he felt the chill creep in when he paused. Even with his woolen hiking shirt, Noah knew he'd have to wear his jacket on the way down. He heard laughing and wisps of conversation above him. He kept walking, expecting to meet the Trump party coming down. A sparrow called to his silent mate as evening approached. No one came down the trail. No voices. *When they spotted me, did they hide behind the hemlocks? Why would they do that? To scare me? I'd expect a dirty trick like that from Trump people.* He began to worry. It was a trick Noah had played on his children, and then his grandchildren: walking ahead, hiding behind a tree or boulder, surprising them when they hurried past. When he last climbed Ampersand with them five years ago, Noah had trouble keeping up with his progeny; they could have played the trick on him, but never did.

He soon reached an easy stretch of about twenty-five yards that ended in a steep staircase, the rock slab of each step implanted by trail crews not long ago. Far ahead, he caught a glimpse of three people, their backs to him, going up the stairs just before the trail curved out of sight. Startled, Noah realized he had been wrong; the laughing voices were not coming down, they were going up. The first two miles to the clearing had been flat, without many roots or rocks to impede progress. Since those ahead of Noah had encountered the rough, steep terrain first, he had gained on them.

He continued at a steady pace up the stairs, his face cast downward, concentrating on the rock slabs. Out of breath by the time he approached the top, he slowed down.

"Hey, grandfather!" an unmistakably female voice hailed him. He glanced up. Two men were sitting on level trail just beyond the steps; the woman was standing between them.

Grandfather? Stopping on the top step, Noah turned around, expecting to see an old man with a flowing white beard trudging up the path, leaning on a gnarled walking stick. He had grown a beard years ago but shaved it off because it made him look old. He still couldn't understand how vendors gave him a senior discount without asking his age.

They looked in their twenties, shabbily dressed, the men in torn jeans with two or three days of stubble on their cheeks. He felt his own cheek and realized he had forgotten to shave for at least two days. One of them wore a sweaty T-shirt inscribed with M*A*G*A across the front; the other's advertised a local brewery. *Are these Hillary's deplorables?* A little taller than Sarah, the girl wore a low-cut halter, short jean shorts, and beat up sneakers with turned-down socks. She had lustrous black hair under her baseball cap, inviting cleavage, firm thighs, and muscular mud-speckled legs. When he reached her, he looked into her piercing dark eyes, appreciating her long lashes, straight nose, well-shaped lips, and smooth, slightly flushed cheeks. "Are you all right, grandfather?" she asked with concern.

Her greeting was not what he would have expected from a Trump person. Still catching his breath, he answered defensively, "Why shouldn't

I be?"

"Well, you're a little old to be climbing alone."

He could have explained that he preferred to hike with his wife but she had been injured. Instead he said, "I'm not that old."

"Maybe. But I hope I can still climb when I'm your age." She turned to her companions, "Come on guys, we gotta keep going if we're gonna get to the top before sunset." One of the men offered Noah a drink from his water bottle.

"No thanks, I've got my own." *I wouldn't drink out of his bottle even if he paid me,* Noah thought to himself as he followed, falling farther behind them. The trail seemed to end at a large, dangerously slanted boulder; Noah tossed his trekking poles ahead and hauled himself up the boulder's smooth surface. When younger, he'd walked up the slab, but after Sarah's fall and his own near misses, he crawled up on his hands and knees, retrieving his poles near the top. Standing, he looked at his watch. Five o'clock. *If I make the top in half an hour, don't linger, go faster on the way down, I'll be back at the trailhead around seven, our dinner time. Sarah will be starting to worry.* But he was getting tired and he still had several steep pitches. *Who am I kidding?* With fatigue and fear of falling, he knew it would take at least as long to get down as it would to get to the top. *If I had obeyed Sarah and set a turn-around time, it would be now.*

The breeze picked up, sometimes sounding as loud as rushing water then dying to a murmur, becoming silent as evening approached. Noah reached the base of an eight-foot-high rock cliff, which he did not remember. *Have I lost the trail?* He retraced his steps for a few feet; the trail was unmistakable even in the growing gloom but narrowed as it moved along the cliff's base. On the far side, the path turned steeply upward along the cliff's edge. Bending down to peer at the ground, he saw the regular indentations of sneakers and hiking boots with a smear where someone had slipped. Carefully planting the tips of his poles in the dirt and moss, he started to clamber up the incline. He planted his right trekking pole in the soft earth halfway up. As he shifted his weight on to it, the pole slipped and Noah lost his balance. He fell to the right, his poles flailing uselessly in the air, scraping his side on the rocky edge of the cliff as he tumbled uncontrollably to the base.

He lay along the trail, wondering if he was hurt. His arms and legs seemed intact. As he tried to get up, he noticed that his shirttail was no longer tucked into his hiking pants and had a small tear. Beneath his shirt, the skin over the ribs on his left side was bruised, slowly oozing blood. *How am I going to explain this to Sarah?* Only when he tried to stand did he realize that his side ached. *I must have cracked a rib or two.* One of his hiking poles, bent slightly in his fall, lay alongside him; the other lay on the far side of the trail. With considerable pain he retrieved it. The notion of continuing upward nauseated him. *That settles it. I've got to turn around.* He put his hands through the loop straps of his poles, noticing immediately that his right wrist hurt when he grabbed the pole. With great difficulty he headed down at a very slow pace, easing himself down the steep boulder, stopping at the head of the rock staircase, uncertain that he had the strength to go on. His watch said six-thirty. The sun had just set. *A little food and drink might help,* he thought hopefully. From his pack he pulled out one of the sandwiches and his water bottle. While he was eating, he heard the girl and her two friends coming down the trail. Once again, she greeted him, "Hey grandfather, are you all right?"

While he chewed, he decided that there was no point in complaining—*they're not going to help me anyway*—but then he thought better of it. "Not exactly. I slipped and fell down the side of the cliff back there. Decided to turn around."

She knelt down next to him. He showed her his right hand. To his surprise the wrist was swollen. She touched it gingerly, evincing a wince.

"Anything else?"

"I may have cracked a couple of ribs. It may take six weeks but they'll heal on their own. That's happened to me before."

"Well, you can't wait for that to happen on the mountain, can you?" she asked with a chuckle. "We'll help you down, hoping we can all get out while there's still light. By the way, what's your name? Mine's Laura. These guys are Jim and Pete."

"Noah."

"Noah? I learned a song about Noah when I was a kid:

'Old man Noah knew a thing or two,
He thought he knew it all…
Some say he was an also ran

He was the original circus man.
Old man Noah…'"

"Not that one," Noah laughed. "I'm not that old." He realized he could no longer put any weight on his right hand or arm. "Would you mind carrying my trekking stick?" he asked Laura sheepishly.

"No problem," she replied. She took it in her right hand, held Noah's right arm with her left, and helped him stand. Pete walked close by Noah's left side where the trail was wide enough for three. The light was growing fainter every minute. "If we don't get down soon, Laura," Jim said, "we're gonna spend the night on the mountain."

"Didn't you think to bring a flashlight?" Noah asked scornfully.

Pete replied, "No cell phones, no flashlight."

"Why not?" Noah asked, as if a cellphone was every person's birthright.

"Can't afford it," Pete answered.

"The deep state doesn't care about us," Jim added. "Neither Pete nor I can find work, and Laura barely ekes out a living as a nurse's aide. There's no cellular up here or where we live."

The deep state? What is he talking about? Noah wondered. "The deep state?" he asked out loud.

"You know, the people who run the country. To Hillary we're just deplorables."

They reached the clearing at eight o'clock in twilight. "Why didn't one of us bring a flashlight?" Laura asked. They sat side by side on a rotting log. Noah took off his pack and dug inside. "My wife was worried I wouldn't make it as fast as I used to and put a head lamp in my pack." He pulled it out and handed it to Laura. "She put sandwiches in there, too. I ate one, but if any of you want the other—"

"No, thank you," Laura replied. "She made it for you and you should have it."

"No," Noah objected. "It'll spoil my appetite for dinner. Why don't you guys share it."

"Thanks, but not now. Let's wait until we get out and then we'll see."

Laura started to put the headlamp on Noah. "No, it'll be safer if one of you wears it," he argued. Pete pulled it on his forehead and walked slowly into the darkness, making sure that the others stayed close to the lamp's beam. The terrain was much easier below the clearing and fairly wide except for the planks, which they walked over in single file.

As they approached the trailhead in total darkness, they saw a light coming toward them. The beam of Pete's headlamp picked up the broad-brimmed hat of a state trooper. "Is one of you Noah?" the trooper asked.

"That's me. Is something wrong, Officer?" Noah responded.

"Only you're being a couple of hours overdue. Are you all right?"

"Not quite," Laura answered. "This gentleman had a fall, probably fractured a rib and sprained his wrist. We're helping him down."

"Can he drive?" the trooper asked. "Or should I radio for an ambulance?"

"Of course I can drive," Noah answered

angrily. The others remained silent.

"Well, I've got another call, so I'll leave you with these folks, Noah. You're lucky they were on the trail." He turned and headed out.

Noah insisted on signing out in the trail register. The time was nine o'clock. They crossed to the parking lot where Pete swept the beam of the headlamp across both cars. "Hey man, I didn't know you were a Sanders bro. Too bad he lost the nomination."

Surprised by Pete's sympathy for his fallen candidate, Noah asked, "So who are you going to vote for in November?"

"We can't vote for the deep state," Jim answered.

"Anyone but Hillary," Laura added. "Where are you headed, Noah?"

"Lake Clear, just off Route 30."

"That's not far out of our way. We'll follow you."

Noah started to protest, but his wrist stabbed with pain when he flexed it and he decided against it. Pete handed the headlamp back to Noah, who popped the Camry's trunk, and dropped his equipment in. Laura climbed into the truck on the driver side; Pete and Jim got in on the passenger side.

Turning the Camry's ignition was painful, but the car started right up. Noah backed out, gripping the wheel firmly with his left hand. He passed the curvy short cut to Route 30 and made the turn directly on to it a mile farther down the road.

On the drive home, he debated what to

tell Sarah. *Should I tell her I didn't make it to the top?* He decided he wouldn't say one way or the other unless she asked. His thoughts turned to Laura and her companions. When he approached
the driveway to his cottage, he put on his left signal. Laura responded by flicking her brights up and down. He turned off, and she drove on.

*

The anger that suffused Sarah's face when she heard Noah drive up evaporated as he walked in, his right arm folded against his chest as if in a sling, his shirttail hanging out and torn. "You're hurt." Gently, she guided him to a kitchen chair. He put his arms on the table; his right wrist was swollen, black and blue. "You fell," she observed, phrased neither as a question nor an accusation. Across the table, his usual place was set, and his and Sarah's dinner plates were covered with aluminum foil.

"Yeah, cracked a rib or two slamming into the side of a cliff," he said.

"I'll put the plates back in the oven to warm them. It will only take a few minutes." After completing the task, she helped Noah get up. "Let's go to the bathroom and clean you up." He obeyed. She undid the buttons on his shirt, slipped it off, and helped him wash his hands. With a soapy washcloth, she gently cleansed the bruise on his side, rinsing it with warm water. Rummaging in the medicine cabinet she found a sterile gauze pad and adhesive tape to cover his chest wound. She got him a clean shirt and helped him button it.

They returned to the kitchen table, where

she served him. "You know, Sarah, I'd really like a cold beer."

"You're lucky, we've got one left." She got it from the refrigerator, opened it, and poured it straight into a chilled glass, so the beer foamed up; Noah liked to smell and sip the head. Realizing he might not appreciate an offer to cut his food, Sarah silently slid his plate toward her and cut most of his chicken off the bones and into small pieces. "You can pick the rest off the bones with your hands. You're allowed."

"Do you think we should stop at the hospital on the way out to see if I broke my wrist?"

Sarah thought about it. "I think right after supper we should wrap it with some ice and see if the swelling goes down. Maybe you should take a couple of Motrin. We can decide in the morning. Whether it's broken or not, I can do the driving."

When they were halfway through the meal, she said, "I called the state police you know."

"Yeah, I know."

"The trooper rescued you?"

"No, we were almost out when he showed up."

"We?" she asked suspiciously.

"Three kids—I guess they're in their twenties, locals I think."

"You hiked with them?" she asked, surprised but relieved.

"No, only after I fell."

"Was that coming down?"

He evaded Sarah's question. "They met me coming down, stayed with me, and followed me as I drove home, making sure I made it safely."

He picked up the chicken bone. "That surprised me."

"Why?"

"They were Trump people, but they certainly weren't deplorable."

"I hope you thanked them."

Noah put the bone down and looked at Sarah. "Thanked them?" Morosely, he thought of Laura's lights flicking up and down, acknowledging his turn into the driveway. *Before I left the parking lot, I should have invited them in, or, at the least, thanked them.* He'd never have another chance

A Foot in the Door

I got home before Eleanor, brought in the mail—usually her chore—and sat on one of the kitchen stools separating the bills from the form letters, advertisements, and catalogs. One letter puzzled me. Was it another piece of junk mail or a genuine personal letter? My name and address were handwritten in blue ink on the pale green envelope. The name V. Green and an address in Walnut Creek, California, were printed on a return address sticker. The letter had a first class "Forever" stamp and bore a Walnut Creek post mark. I did not know any V. Green, nor anyone in Walnut Creek, and I was about to add it to the junk pile when I noticed the handwriting looked familiar. I opened the envelope, retrieving two sheets of pale green stationery folded horizontally, with writing on both sides in the same hand and ink as the address. The salutation, "Dear Dr. W.," and the signature, "Vicky," instantly identified the sender.

Eleanor's car pulled into the carport. Quickly, I scooped up all the bills and junk mail, put them on top of the green letter and empty envelope, grabbed my keys, and went upstairs, where I shoved all the mail in the top drawer of my desk. I went back downstairs.

"You just get home?" Eleanor asked. "I thought I heard you going up the stairs. Did you get the mail?"

"No, I was just going out to check." Walking halfway down the driveway to the mailbox, which was mounted on an old oak tree, I peered in and slammed it shut. "No mail," I reported.

"We're supposed to be at the Johnsons for dinner at seven o'clock, so we'd better get ready."

After Eleanor left for her law firm the next morning, I finally opened the desk drawer and retrieved Vicky's letter. I had not slept well, worrying about its contents, but I did not get out of bed for fear of waking Eleanor.

> *Dear Dr. W.,*
>
> *It's been twenty-seven years since we were last in contact, but the #MeToo movement and the Kavanaugh debacle have activated the dormant anger. You have no idea of the misfortunes that befell me after I left your employ. I'm not quite sure whether I can quench my anger, but informing you is the first step….*

Never in my life had I confronted danger with helplessness, but Vicky's letter knocked the air out of me. On the few occasions when I had thought about her in the ensuing years, I had to admit that I acted foolishly. It never occurred to me I would be called to account.

*

Thirty years ago, I was appointed to the research faculty at Bates-Bronsted Medical School in Virginia and given my own lab, complete with start-up funds to use until my grant applications were approved. The Human Resources Department sent me the names of five applicants for the technician position. Three were far superior and I arranged separate interviews with them. The male applicant was not a long-term prospect as he expected to go to graduate school in a few years. The two women both expected to stay in the job longer and were equally qualified. Both had baccalaureate degrees. I decided to hire Vicky, the less attractive one. Since marrying Eleanor three years earlier I had never looked at another woman but working in close proximity to an attractive technician might have tempted me.

Victoria's figure was cloaked in loose blouses and slacks, further hidden by a long lab coat. She had shoulder-length dirty blonde hair and wore eyeglasses for nearsightedness. They had oval, turquoise frames that matched her eyes and she frequently pushed them up her small nose. Though free of blemishes, her face had the look of fine sandpaper. Her mouth and chin were not noteworthy.

The lab had two bays; Vicky worked at one, I at the other. She addressed me as "Dr. W.," which I never corrected to "Fred," though I called her "Vicky."

With Vicky's help, my research made great progress and I was promoted to associate professor ahead of schedule. Her contribution warranted making her a co author on two papers, which were published in prestigious molecular biology journals.

In late spring toward the end of Vicky's second year, the department's senior professor invited the faculty, postdoc fellows, and technicians, with their spouses, to a Saturday evening party. He and his wife lived in a large stone house on top of a hill in one of the wealthier suburbs. A spacious lawn sloped downward from a flat patio on which a temporary bar had been erected. The guests stood in small knots, leaving the scattered garden chairs empty. The affair was catered and circulating waiters served hors d'oeuvres. Lanterns had been hung from the few trees on the lawn, and floodlights on the rear wall of the house illuminated the patio. Eleanor and I were already there, holding our drinks and chatting with one of my colleagues and his wife, when Vicky and her husband came out from the house led by our host's wife. They looked around bewildered and I excused myself to greet them.

"Hi, Dr. W. This is my husband, Peter." We shook hands. I already knew his name from conversations with Vicky, and that he worked for a large insurance firm. They had married the year before Vicky came to work for me, renting a one-bedroom apartment in one of the less affluent suburbs, postponing children until they could afford a home of their own. Peter's face was scarred from healed acne and his voice was slightly nasal. He shook hands limply with a moist palm.

I had never seen Vicky in a dress before. Tight fitting and black, with the hem falling just above her knees, it revealed shapely legs, a slender waist, and a pleasing bust. Eleanor, who had never met Vicky, walked over and I introduced them. The four of us talked until one of the other technicians in the department greeted Vicky, and Eleanor and I wandered away. But I could not help sneaking glances at Vicky. On the way home that evening, Eleanor commented, "Your technician has quite a figure, don't you think?"

"I hadn't noticed," I lied.

The following Monday in the lab, I asked Vicky if she and Peter had had a good time at the staff party. She said yes and described some of the people they had talked to. "That was a lovely dress you were wearing," I added.

"Oh, thank you. I bought it for the occasion." She then went about her work as I wrote up an experiment.

One extremely hot day that summer, I happened to be in the lab when Vicky arrived wearing a tight-fitting jersey and miniskirt. She put on her lab coat and went to work. I was also in the lab when she removed her lab coat eight hours later. She looked lovely, but I decided not to compliment her. On the way home, I realized that Vicky's body was distracting me. Eleanor and I were happily married and enjoyed sex together. But I was like a kid wanting a new toy. What harm could there be in having it? Eleanor would be furious if she found out, but as long as I did not change my behavior, there was little chance she would. What had come over me? How could I work two years alongside Vicky without ever having a lecherous thought and then change instantly because of a tight dress?

One of the professional societies I belonged to held its annual scientific meeting in the fall. In order to present their work, scientists had to submit abstracts by September 1st. I asked Vicky to draft an abstract on work she had executed and placed her name on it as first author. When the abstract was accepted, I asked if she wanted to go to New York City to present the paper. She was thrilled. "I've never been there and always wanted to go." She hesitated. "Do you think I'm knowledgeable enough to answer questions after my talk?"

"As well as I could," I answered. "Besides, I'll be in the audience and can expand on what you say, but I doubt it will be necessary." I told Eleanor that I was taking Vicky to New York, explaining that technicians occasionally presented papers.

I registered us for the meeting, reserving two rooms in the hotel in which it would be held. On the appointed day, I picked Vicky up at her home and we drove the five hours to New York. Early in the trip, I asked Vicky to talk out her presentation without slides or script, which she did very well. When she finished, the conversation became more personal. Peter was eager to start a family, she told me, laughingly pointing out that birth control was in her hands, something I had wondered about. I described our grown kids' accomplishments, as well as Eleanor's, implying we had a happy marriage. Vicky didn't say that anything was wrong with her marriage; she just thought they needed more financial security before having kids.

I turned to her momentarily. "I guess that means you'll be with me for a while longer."

"I don't mind. I enjoy working in your lab much more than I expected when I started."

"I enjoy working with you, too, Vicky." Again, I looked at her briefly. "I didn't expect when I hired you that I would become as fond of you as I have."

"Thank you," she said innocently, looking straight ahead.

The propitious moment had arrived. "So fondly," I continued, "that I'd like us to have an affair." Bang! The cat was out of the bag.

This time, she did turn her head. Pretending to be intent on driving, I did not turn to read her face.

The traffic had picked up as we approached the city and I had to concentrate on switching lanes to get off the highway and then maneuver on to another highway to get into the Lincoln Tunnel. Once in Manhattan I had to search for our hotel. My proposition was left hanging.

We arrived about five in the afternoon as twilight approached, and I parked my car in the hotel garage. We carried our bags to the lobby and checked in. A bellhop gathered the bags and led us to our respective rooms, which were on the sixth floor but not adjacent. We came to Vicky's room first. I whispered that I would take care of the tip and then said out loud, "Why don't we meet in the lobby in half an hour. The society is having an opening reception, which I, uhh, we, should go to."

Had Vicky not heard my proposition? Was she pretending not to have heard? Maybe she thought I wouldn't bring it up again. I called the concierge and got a recommendation for a quiet, romantic restaurant and asked him to make a dinner reservation for two at seven.

At the reception, I ran into two men with whom I had done postdocs and we started to catch up on each other's news. Vicky arrived, standing idly by until one of the men turned to her and asked, "Are you a postdoc with Fred?"

I introduced her. "Vicky is my senior technician. She's presenting our paper tomorrow." I did not let on that she was my only technician. We got into a discussion about her work, and she handled their questions expertly. A female colleague in my department joined us and we chatted until the reception started to break up. "Hey," one of the men said, "why don't we go out to dinner together. There's a new Thai place that's supposed to be terrific."

The others, including Vicky, were enthusiastic. Reluctantly, I had to go along with the plan. My friends would know something was going on if I told them that Vicky and I had made other arrangements. We all agreed to meet in the lobby at a quarter to seven.

From my room, I called the concierge to cancel the reservation. When I came back to the lobby, Vicky was standing alone wearing the same black dress that had allured me at the staff party. The others soon joined us.

Dinner with the group was fun, although I had no opportunity to speak to Vicky alone. We got back to the hotel a little before ten; she and I were the only ones to get out of the elevator on the sixth floor. As we approached her door, she opened her purse to get her room key. In a low voice I asked, "You did hear what I said to you in the car?"

Her head was down, looking for the key. "About an affair?"

"Yes."

"I didn't think you were serious."

"I was very serious."

She found the key and inserted it into the door lock. "Dr. W., I enjoy working with you but I'm married, and I've been brought up to think adultery is a sin." She inserted the key, opened the door, walked through it, put her hand on the inner knob, and turned to face me. "I promised to call Peter. I also want to go over my talk one more time. Good night, Dr. W. I had a lovely evening," she said and then started to close the door. I put my foot on the threshold, preventing the door from closing. Vicky opened it wider, wondering why it would not close until she saw my foot. I pushed her into the room and walked past her. The door closed automatically, and she turned toward me. Backing her into the door, I grasped her shoulders and kissed her. For a moment she was rigid and resistant. Then, to my astonishment, she melted. I felt her body relax and we clung together until she eased out of my grip.

"That wasn't so terrible, was it?" I asked.

"I've never done anything like this before. I'm sorry."

"Why are you apologizing?"

"I'm not that sort of girl. I'm a happily married woman."

"Look Vicky, I've told you I've grown fond of you. I hoped you felt the same way about me. We're both happily married and can continue to be."

She looked up at me—I couldn't tell whether with sadness or fright. "I promised to call Peter before I went to bed."

*

You'll never know how rapidly my heart was beating when you put your foot in the door and forced your way into my hotel room in New York. I had hoped that my silence after your proposition would tell you that I was not interested.

When you pinned me against the door, all I could think about was how to fend you off. The thought occurred to me that maybe a passionate kiss would satisfy you. When you asked, "Now that wasn't so bad, was it?" I thought that would be the end of it. When you left willingly, I was relieved.

As you will recall, my talk the next morning went well. Afterward, a professor at another university asked if I was interested in a junior faculty slot. I was euphoric but told him I was committed to you for at least another year, without letting on that I was a technician. After the coffee break, I had a hard time concentrating on the talks. Famished before the morning sessions ended, I left early, found a small sandwich shop on Sixth Avenue, and had lunch by myself at the counter. After I ordered, my thoughts wandered. Maybe I should get a Ph.D., as you had once suggested. That would infuriate Peter; his career was going nowhere, and I'd become the major breadwinner. Despite my annual salary raises, it would be years before I could afford to quit a full-time job though, let alone pay tuition.

*

"Can you manage on your own for lunch?" I asked Vicky at the coffee break after her talk. "I've got a committee meeting to attend." Perhaps wishfully, I thought a look of disappointment crossed her face.

"Of course I can," she answered quickly. We agreed to meet for dinner.

*

After what you did the second night, I wasn't sure I wanted to work for you any longer. But I worried that you wouldn't give me a good reference after being rebuffed, which I was sure I would do if you persisted. On the other hand, maybe your passion was based on love, despite your rough approach and sudden departure. This seemed unlikely though; you said you were happily married, and I took you at your word. Then again, I told you I was happily married when I was already harboring doubts about Peter.

*

We walked to the quiet restaurant the concierge had recommended the previous day. A few steps below street level, the dimly lit restaurant had only eight small tables covered with red-checkered cloths. Those that were occupied were lit by candles, and as we sat down the waiter lit ours. "Shall we order a bottle of wine?"

Vicky looked frightened. "You're not trying to get me drunk, are you?"

"Why would I do that?" I asked, laughing lightly. I ordered a demi-liter and started questioning Vicky about what she had learned at the other sessions. The food was good and with the wine the conversation flowed sweetly and politely. Worried that she might have told her husband about my advance the previous night, I asked if she had talked to Peter. "He wasn't home when I first called," she said, "but he answered just before I was going to turn the light out. He was playing poker with his buddies."

"Do you believe him?" I asked, trying to sow seeds of doubt that might accrue to my advantage.

"Sure I do. He told me he broke even."

As on the previous night, we walked to her door together. As she put the key in the lock, I asked, "May I come in?"

"I promised to call Peter."

"Good idea, Eleanor will want to hear how your talk went." I retreated to my room.

Eleanor reported on her day before asking how Vicky's presentation went.

"Very well," I replied. "She even got a job offer afterwards."

"That's nice. Will she take it?"

"The professor who offered it mistook her for a postdoc, but she didn't let on. She just told him she was committed to me for another year."

"Clever woman. And good looking, too."

We must have spoken for about fifteen minutes but as soon as I got off the phone, I walked down the hall and knocked on Vicky's door.

"Who is it?" she asked.

"Fred."

Having already put the chain across the door, she peered out through the small opening. "I was just getting ready for bed." She held up her toothbrush as proof. "It's been a long day."

"Did you get Peter?"

"Yes, I think I woke him up. He said he can't wait for me to get home."

"Do you mind if I come in for a minute."

"I'm already in my pajamas."

"I don't mind." Vicky sighed as she unhooked the chain. Her loose cotton pajamas revealed the soft outline of her breasts. We stood facing each other alongside the bed. "I thought I'd give you a goodnight kiss." I took a step closer. She looked distressed as I put my hands on her shoulders, drew her near, and kissed her. As on the previous night, she resisted but then melted. After a few moments we were sitting on her bed, and soon we were lying side by side on top of the covers. As we continued a deep-throated kiss, I pulled her pajama top loose and massaged her back. Her skin had the texture of fine sandpaper, like her face, comparing unfavorably to Eleanor's silky smooth skin. I paused to take my pants off and then pulled her pajama bottoms down.

"Do you mind if I turn off the light?" Vicky asked.

"Is that the way you and Peter do it?" I answered with a snicker.

Without replying she reached over and switched off the lamp.

"Are you going to put something on?" she asked matter of factly.

"I thought you were on the pill."

"I am but maybe we should be double safe."

Rolling on top of her, I replied, "I don't have a condom. Everything will be fine."

Instantly after my spasm of ecstasy, I was overwhelmed by a tsunami of revulsion, of self-loathing; my attraction to Vicky dissipated in an instant and I withdrew quickly without thinking whether she had climaxed. "That was very nice," I lied, pulling my undershorts on. Vicky got out of bed, found her pajamas, and went to the bathroom. When she came out, I was fully dressed, ready to leave. I kissed her lightly on the lips, said goodnight without making plans to meet in the morning, and let myself out.

We drove back to Virginia the next day, a Friday, not having much conversation on the way. I dropped Vicky at her door, came home, and greeted Eleanor with a big kiss. We made love that night with no revulsion on my part.

*

It was about six-thirty when you dropped me off. Peter was sitting in front of the television, holding a beer in one hand with two empties on the floor beside him. "I thought you'd be home in time to make dinner," he grumbled belligerently. I didn't remember saying that.

He tottered to his feet and grabbed my wrist. "Were you screwing your boss?" he asked menacingly.

"What gave you that idea?" I replied as innocently as possible.

He pulled me close to him and kissed me roughly. When I tried to back away, he tightened his grip. "My kiss isn't good enough for you anymore?" He flung me across the room, I stumbled, and as I fell my cheek struck the wooden arm of one of our chairs, just below my eye. Grabbing my wrist, he pulled me up and marched me to the bathroom. "Where are your pills?" I looked at him anxiously as he started to twist my arm. "You know what I mean—your birth control pills." I told him they were in my toilet kit. Releasing his grip, he commanded me to get them. Dutifully, I opened the valise, returned to the bathroom, and handed them to him. Tearing the pack open, he tossed the pills into the toilet and flushed. He dragged me to the bedroom and started to take his shirt off. "Are you waiting for me to rip your clothes off?" I can only call what happened next rape.

By Saturday I had a good shiner despite using ice as soon as I had the opportunity. Peter was sober and apologized for how he had manhandled me. He did not ask any more questions but did say that now I was off the pill we'd soon have a family. I knew that if I started to take the pills surreptitiously, he'd beat me when he discovered it.

The swelling had gone but the area under my eye was still black and blue on Monday morning. I knew I couldn't lie about how it happened, but I didn't want you to think my marriage was collapsing and I was easy prey. Prey is the right word; I felt caught *between two predators. So I stayed home wondering whether you'd call, and if you did, what I would say.*

*

Vicky did not come to work on Monday. She had never missed a day without telling me in advance or calling. Had she decided to quit without giving notice? She was in the middle of a pay period and would forfeit her last earnings.

I went to the weekly staff conference and a talk by a prominent visiting scientist but had a hard time concentrating. Despite my self-loathing after sex with Vicky, I began to crave her again. Should I call her? Maybe she was sick and my calling would show my concern. On the other hand, it might indicate that I cared for her more than I really did. If she really had quit abruptly, I had no way of talking her out of it.

When I arrived on Tuesday Vicky was already in the lab, wearing sunglasses instead of her regular ones, setting up an experiment we had planned before the New York excursion. We stayed out of each other's way until five o'clock, when Vicky was getting ready to leave. I was sitting at our joint desk when, uninvited, she pulled up a chair alongside it. "Peter got a promotion last week. With that and the raises you've given me, we've decided to start a family. I've gone off the pill."

"Are you pregnant?"

"Not that fast," she smiled.

Gently holding her arm, I lied and said, "I'm happy for you." Our trip to New York never came up.

Vicky announced she was pregnant five months later and worked until her eighth month.

The next part of Vicky's letter stunned me.

*

In my eighth month, Peter announced he was leaving me for another woman and suggested that I put the baby up for adoption. He moved out and sued for divorce on the grounds of adultery. When I told the judge that the only extramarital relationship I had had was forced on me and ended three months before I became pregnant, he told Peter he'd have to find other grounds for a divorce unless I agreed to it.

I wasn't as fortunate with child support; Peter denied he was the father and DNA testing to prove it was not yet available. Two weeks before I delivered, I moved in with my mother in Maryland. My father had abandoned her many years ago and she had scraped together enough to live on as a teacher's assistant until she was asked to retire a few months earlier. Between us we had enough to live on for about six months after Lucy was born. I started to look for work when she was three months old but was reluctant to go back to you or use your name as a reference. I tried several hospitals in D.C. and Baltimore and was told either that I was over-trained or under-qualified. Going on, welfare loomed large. We started to skimp on food and Lucy, whom I was breastfeeding, fell below the third percentile at her six-month exam. I saw an ad for a laboratory technician at NIH and reluctantly decided to list you, and the papers on which you put my name, in my application. I never knew whether you were contacted, but I got the job and was able to support Lucy and my mother, who served as her babysitter. When my boss accepted a professorship at UC Berkeley, he offered to take me and another technician with him. Lucy was only two, and despite the promise of a higher salary I couldn't imagine uprooting my mother and couldn't afford to take Lucy without her. It took almost a year before I found another job. Then my mother had a stroke, and I had to care for her until a second stroke killed her, about six months after the first.

I started to drink out of loneliness and lost one job after another when I didn't show up for work. I joined Alcoholics Anonymous, where one of the few women told me about a women's self-help group. I felt much more comfortable talking to them about my downfall than to AA. I learned that the chain reaction unleashed by your harassment of me was not unique.

By then, Lucy was in school and coping better than her mother. We moved in with another woman who had a daughter a few years older than Lucy. We all became very close. Her family lived in California and we decided to pool our meager savings to travel across country and try our luck there. I finally divorced Peter and reverted to my maiden name, Green. I contacted my old boss at NIH, who hired me for his lab at Berkeley.

For all I know, you may have left the university by now, so I've decided to write you at home. Please let me know if you receive this letter.

Vicky

*

I folded the letter, put it back in its envelope, and sat staring out the window. The day had turned from sunny to overcast. "The times they are a-changin'," I said to myself. In those days, extramarital affairs were an open secret to all but the wives, and sometimes even to them. I thought about two of my colleagues, both happily married I presumed. One would lock himself in his office with his secretary for indecent amounts of time; she went in with lipstick on and came out with none. A postdoctoral fellow told me once that my department chair had propositioned her but she had declined as politely as she could. I could think of more examples.

The irony of what I had done struck me. Ever since I learned that my father had made it clear he didn't want my mother to work, I had vowed not to impose that dictum on my wife or wish it on other women. I had insisted that Eleanor go to law school, encouraged her to keep her maiden name, fostered her career, given preference to women candidates for faculty positions, and supported their advancement up the academic ladder. And imposed my lust on Vicky.

The kid with the new toy. Once, long ago, I had carelessly broken a new toy my parents had given me. I gathered up the pieces and hid them where I was sure my mother would never find them. Of course, she did. The lecture she gave me afterward was not about breaking the toy but keeping my guilt secret. Now I had another secret. This time, I was not the only one in on it. What would Vicky do? What should I do?

When I can't settle on a course of action, even related to my scientific work, I often consult Eleanor. Telling her about Vicky might threaten our marriage. On the other hand, if Vicky made a public accusation, or maybe wrote to Eleanor directly, her reaction could be much worse.

She soon decided the strategy for me. Over coffee that night, she commented that I had been awfully quiet during dinner. "Come to think of it," she added, "you were awfully quiet at the Johnsons' last night."

"Was I?"

"Are you preoccupied with a problem at the lab? Or is it something else?"

I pushed my chair back. "Stay here. I'll be right back." I returned and handed her the pale green envelope.

She looked at the address. "When did this come?"

"Yesterday."

"I thought you said there was no mail." I shrugged.

She extracted the letter, unfolded it, retrieved reading glasses from her handbag, and read quietly as I finished my coffee and began to clear the table. Twice she glanced at me but said nothing before returning to the letter. When she finished, she folded the letter, inserted it back in the envelope, and held it up. "Is what she says true?"

"The part about me is. I can't attest to the rest."

"Your part is what I meant." She took off her glasses. "Why are you showing this to me?"

"You're my wife, and I don't know what to do."

"Your wife? Your wife?" Eleanor's voice rose. "You hand me a letter from a woman whom you hoodwinked into going to New York with you, whom you essentially raped, and you never bothered to tell me until she confronted you, and now you want me to tell you what to do?"

"I wish you wouldn't call it rape. She did consent, you know."

"Under duress."

She handed the envelope back to me and sat drinking her coffee plaintively. "To tell you the truth, Fred, I had my suspicions. After I met Vicky at the staff party and you told me on the way home that you hadn't noticed how attractive she was, I wondered. And then when you admitted it was unusual for a technician to present a paper, I grew more suspicious. Your call from New York, before or after you raped her, assuaged my worries but when you told me five months later that Vicky was pregnant, I grew alarmed, relieved only when she still hadn't had the baby eleven months after your trip to New York."

Eleanor took her cup to the sink, poured dish detergent in the tub, and turned on the hot water. Quickly, she shut it off and turned to the table where I sat restively. "Are you fearful of what she's going to do to you or remorseful of what you did to her? The shoe is on the other foot now, isn't it? It's no longer yours in her door."

I did not answer, afraid to admit that I feared what Vicky would do to me.

Eleanor picked up her coffee cup, returned to the table, and refilled it. "Did you ever think back then about how you might be putting Vicky in harm's way, aside from the small chance of pregnancy?" Looking squarely into my eyes, she waited for an answer.

I answered truthfully. "No."

Eleanor took a long swallow. "Well, Fred, if you want me to tell you what to do, the first thing I'd say is apologize—"

"Of course. I'm sorry for what I did to you."

"You didn't let me finish." She put her cup down. "The first thing I'd say is apologize to Vicky."

"Won't that be an admission of guilt?"

"You are guilty."

"What could she do to me?"

"Nothing under the statute of limitations. But you're evading your guilt, Fred. You're not thinking of the harm you caused—her husband beating her, raping her, leaving her single and jobless after having his baby. Then her becoming an alcoholic until a relationship with a woman saved her." Eleanor got up from the table and started to walk to the sink. She stopped abruptly as if a new idea had hit her, returned to her seat, and looked penetratingly at me. "Were there others?"

"Only one." The affair flashed through my mind. Sheila, my secretary for a few years after Vicky, was single and looking for a husband. At first, she said she wasn't interested, doubting I was marriageable, but with a little persistence she agreed. We had many trysts before she met a man she liked, whom she eventually married.

"Did she depend on you for her livelihood as Vicky did?"

"Yes, I suppose she did."

"Suppose? You weren't aware that you were exerting your power over them? Your lust was so strong that it never crossed your mind that Vicky and the other one were dependent on you?"

"Pretty despicable," I admitted. "But you know, Eleanor, working closely with someone toward a common goal, as I did with Vicky, engenders a fondness."

"I understand that." She hesitated. "It's happened to me."

"Really?"

I don't think she meant that to slip out, but she continued. "Not with someone over whom I had power—I would never let that happen—but a colleague I worked closely with on a complicated case several years ago."

"Why didn't you tell me?" I asked.

"Why didn't you tell me?" she shot back.

"Did you fuck him?"

Eleanor got up in disgust. "Is that the most important thing to you? Is that all you men think about?" She sat down again. "No, it didn't go that far. We gained respect for each other and with that came fondness, perhaps love. It might have gone further but neither of us wanted to jeopardize our marriages or hurt our children. Unlike my friend, you couldn't control your desire."

"The dress made a big difference."

"Yes, your fondness erupted into lust."

"You know, Eleanor, as soon as I satisfied myself with Vicky and, uh, the other one, I felt disgusted with myself, revolted by what I had done. It's never been like that when you and I make love."

"I'm glad to hear it. But despite your revulsion you had a craving, like an addiction. Have you gotten over it?"

I had been asking myself that question since Vicky's letter arrived. I had gotten over the use of force. When Eleanor brought home stories of violence against women that her clients had related, I was horrified. I would never do anything like that, I said to myself, forgetting my behavior toward Vicky. I had learned to take "no" for an answer and would never use force again. "Yes," I answered meekly.

"Is that because you can't," which she well knew, "or because it's morally wrong?"

"Both," I said. We sat facing each other, the coffee long gone. Despite her snow-white hair, her face etched with lines, Eleanor appeared to me as she would to no one else: the same piercing green eyes that flashed intelligence and determination, the same nose, the same lips, the same beauty as when we first dated. She returned to the sink, let the hot water run until the dishes were covered, and started to wash them. Taking a towel off its rack, I moved alongside her and started to dry. "Do you think a letter to Vicky with my apology will satisfy her?"

"You won't know until you try. Unless she makes your letter public, you have nothing to lose."

"Do you think she would do that?"

"How would I know?" Having finished the dishes, she turned the water off and dried her hands. "I suppose you could preempt her—issue a public statement yourself."

"How would I do that?"

Eleanor was tiring of our conversation. "I'm sure you can find a way."

"If our kids see it, they'll hate me."

"I doubt that. They've known you all their lives; you're their father, and a loving one." We stood, looking at each other. I took a step toward her and tentatively extended my arms. She started to back away, but then she turned to face me and threw her arms around me. I felt her crying and started to cry, too. When we separated, she wiped away my tears and then hers with the dish towel.

*

Dear Vicky,

Nothing can undo the harm I caused you, but at least I can apologize for the hurt.

I would be horrified if my two sons behaved in the way I did and equally horrified that I might lose their love and trust by openly admitting what I did. But by not speaking out against such behavior, I have fostered it. Unless more men voluntarily come clean, sexual harassment will continue. The #MeToo movement of victims has done much to abate it; a #MeToo movement among perpetrators is also needed.

I'm attaching a letter I have just sent to our local newspaper. I don't know what more I can do.

Sadly,
Fred

Enclosure:

Letter to the Editor, *Richmond Star-Gazette*

This letter is not in reply to a story in the *Richmond Star-Gazette*, although the paper has reported numerous stories on the same subject lately. Rather, I write in regard to a letter I received last week from a woman who worked for me about thirty years ago whom I had not heard from until the #MeToo movement activated the anger that had been lying dormant in her. She had the courtesy to inform me of the source of her anger before deciding what else to do. She was married at the time I asked her to have an affair. She refused and I forced my attention on her.

Neither she nor I have any doubt that my selfish behavior unleashed the calamities that befell her. Her husband beat her and ran off with another woman, leaving her to care for their child without providing support. She had difficulty finding work and became an alcoholic until a women's group rescued her. I have written her to apologize and attached a copy of this letter. People may say that I've done so to forestall more drastic action on her part. I have already told my wife of my transgression, and I could lose my job.

Rather than deny the accusations and persist in immoral sexist activity, men should acknowledge that what they did was hurtful to their victims. In our male-dominated society, it has taken courage for women to come forward and say #MeToo. Now, men must step forward and say, "I too have harassed and/or assaulted." Call it the #IToo movement.

Fred Woolf, Ph.D.
Professor
Bates-Bronsted School of Medicine

The Nobel Prize in Literature

Since the popularization of the Internet, the World
Wide Web, Google, and social media at the dawn of
the new millennium, the mantle of news has spread
farther than ever before. Take sexual misconduct.
Kings, princes, presidents, and others could harass and
cheat with impunity through most of the twentieth
century. Today, not even the Swedish Royal Academy,
which awards most of the Nobel Prizes, can escape the
gaze of these instrumentalities. In 2018, the Academy
did not award the Nobel Prize in Literature after
accusations of sexual harassment and physical abuse
against the husband of an Academy member received
widespread attention. A delay in announcing the award
in 1999, when the instrumentalities mentioned above
were in their infancy or not even born, received scant
attention. I stumbled across the circumstances while
perusing the diaries of the noted American psychiatrist,
Frank Sigman, who died in 2010. Dr. Sigman learned
of the delay from the morning news on National Public
Radio on October 5th, 1999, which I corroborated
from the NPR archives. If what I reconstructed from

Sigman's diaries is true, the story could have caused the Swedish Academy considerable embarrassment had it not been quickly squelched.

*

Dr. Sigman's involvement began when he was awakened by an early morning phone call on October 5th, 1999 from Wilma Rachlik, the night nurse at Hidden Waters, a premier assisted living facility. Nurse Rachlik skipped the pleasantries and got to the point: One of the residents was hallucinating and violent. Wilma had recently taken the job at Hidden Waters to have relative peace and quiet. For the previous twenty years, she had been the head nurse of the psychiatric inpatient unit at University Hospital, where she watched legions of psychiatrists train, thinking most of them incompetent. Frank Sigman was one of them.

When he finished his residency, Frank went into private practice, doing quite nicely as he listened to the well-to-do express their anxieties and depressions. Bored with his patients, he wrote unsolicited op-eds for *The Daily Chronicle* on important mental health issues, pleading, for instance, for better care for people with Alzheimer's disease. After a few of his op-eds were published, he happened to meet the editor at a cocktail party. On the spot, the editor invited Frank to become a regular columnist, writing when the mood struck and receiving modest remuneration. He had been doing so for the past two years while continuing his practice.

Wiping away sleep, Frank asked, "Really violent?"

"You always were one to doubt me, Frank."

Rachlik paused. *Maybe she's going to hang up*, Frank hoped. *Why in hell did she call anyway?* He heard her exasperated sigh. "When a man runs out of his apartment in his underwear at two in the morning, shouting 'I won, I won,' and then throws three books at the night nurse—that's not normal behavior, Frank."

"What did he say he'd won?"

"The Nobel Prize in Literature."

"What's his name?"

"Albert Solnitz."

Frank was gaining consciousness. "The writer?"

"He hasn't written anything since he's been here."

"How long has that been?"

"Five years."

"And how old is he?"

"Ninety-two."

The floor-to-ceiling drapery in Frank's bedroom homogenized day and night. He put his free hand where his partner should have been. *Gone, probably to the club for her tennis game.* "What time is it, Wilma?"

"Six-thirty." Wilma paused. "In the morning."

Frank raised himself on one elbow. "I know it's the morning. Why didn't you phone the staff psychiatrist?"

"Solnitz refuses to talk to him, says there's nothing wrong." Neither of them spoke for a moment.

"I've a busy day, Wilma. What's the rush?"

"He's a danger to himself and the staff, throwing books, screaming, going half-naked in public. I didn't come to Hidden Waters to deal with this kind of behavior."

"Do you think he's psychotic?"

Wilma knew not to overstep the boundary with

Frank. "You're the doctor," she said sarcastically.

Wide awake, Frank realized what she was asking. "You want me to say he's certifiable so you can get rid of him?"

She answered obliquely. "Since he won't talk to the staff psychiatrist, or any psychiatrist for that matter, we don't know how sick he is."

"What makes you think he'll talk to me? I'm a psychiatrist, too."

If Frank could have looked through the line, he would have seen Wilma rolling her eyes as if to ask, *How dense is this man?* "But he doesn't know that, Frank," she said patiently.

Placing the receiver in the crook of his neck, Frank tossed off the covers and sat up, swinging his legs over the side of the bed. With a twinge of hostility, he asked, "Why me, Wilma?"

"Well, with your writing for *The Daily Chronicle* I thought his—" She hesitated.

"Delusion?"

"Whatever you want to call it, Frank. I thought it might interest you."

The phone was on a long cord and now Frank took it off the night table and walked toward the window. "What does my column have to do with it?" he asked.

"I can't tell you how to conduct your work, Frank, but you could play along with him. You could say you're a reporter for *The Daily Chronicle*. That would arrest his suspicions."

"First of all, I am not a reporter."

"*The Chronicle* pays you, doesn't it?" Wilma interrupted.

"That has nothing to do with it. Second, what

you're asking is highly unethical. I could lose my medical license."

He walked the phone back to the night table and sat on his side of the king bed. He began to think: *What if Solnitz won the Nobel Prize? That would be a scoop. Claiming to be a reporter wouldn't be too far off the mark.*

He heard voices close to Wilma's as she replied. "Look, Dolores—the head day nurse— just came in, Frank. I've got to brief her. Can I tell her you'll be in around eight?" Frank grunted. "Great, she'll have Solnitz ready. So long."

Before Frank could utter a word, she hung up.

*

Habit forced Frank to put on a tie, but he picked an old corduroy sports jacket, patched at the elbows, a worn pair of chinos, and his loafers—costume befitting the reporter Wilma had ordained. While dressing, he turned the name over in his mind. *Solnitz, Solnitz.* In the living room, he opened the drapes; the slanted rays of early morning sun illuminated the books arranged by author on the floor-to-ceiling shelves. He pulled out a six-hundred-page tome, *Weary Warrior*, by Albert Solnitz, 1975. The gold disk embossed on the dust jacket announced it had been a finalist for the National Book Award. He read the brief summary and rave reviews on the flaps and the back cover, then re-shelved the book.

In his BMW, he thought, *Why am I doing this? I could get in big trouble. And yet...* To stop his torment, he turned on NPR to listen to the eight o'clock news. After listing the day's casualties in the never-ending wars, Carl Kassell intoned, "According to a spokesman, the Swedish Academy is delaying its announcement of the winner of the Nobel Prize in

Literature, which was expected this morning. No explanation was given." Concluding that this meant that Solnitz could not have won, Frank almost turned around, but then he wondered why there had been a delay and continued his drive to Hidden Waters. Besides, he had made a commitment to Wilma. In the past, he had crossed her at his peril.

At Hidden Waters, Frank parked in the visitors' lot. Avoiding the sprinklers caressing neat rows of chrysanthemums along the paths, he walked to the main building.

The receptionist asked Frank to take a seat. He was surrounded by residents, some reading, a few looking at the overhead television screen, most dozing, like the man sitting next to him, chin on chest, in need of a shave, his open cardigan revealing coffee stains on his shirt. *Could he be Solnitz?* Frank wondered. In a few minutes, a woman in a blue smock emerged from the adjacent office.

Scanning the room for strangers, she greeted Frank with a warm smile. "I'm Dolores. We're glad you came. Wilma really is worried that Albert will harm someone." Two attributes set Dolores apart from Wilma: She was attractive, probably in her late thirties or early forties; and she smiled at him warmly. "I'll let Albert know you're here." She leaned closer to Frank—he liked her perfume—and whispered, "I told him there's a reporter coming to interview him."

Frank picked up a magazine, scanning the pages. In a few minutes, the elevator on the rear wall of the lounge disgorged a man pushing a walker. His thin gray hair was slicked back and parted on the left side. He had on a suit jacket a size too big, with a dress shirt open at the collar. Pushing his walker straight toward Frank, who noticed a few nicks on his shaven face, he asked, "You came to see me?"

As Frank stood, Dolores came up to them. "Have you already met?" she asked.

"He's the reporter, isn't he?" Solnitz asked.

Frank stuck out his hand. "Frank Sigman. You're Albert Solnitz?" Albert grasped Frank's warm hand in his cold clammy one.

"Albert," Dolores said, "why don't you take Frank to the room we use for interviewing applicants? You know where it is." She gave Solnitz a once-over. "You're looking very handsome today, Albert; dressed for the occasion, too." Albert flashed a smile and kissed her cheek.

Pushing his walker, Solnitz led Frank to the room. Frank overtook the walker and opened the door. The room was pleasant: mauve walls provided a soothing background to Renoir and Cezanne reproductions, accompanied by plush, wall-to-wall carpeting in a lighter shade. The one window in the wall opposite the door faced a large courtyard with a well-kept lawn and lawn chairs encircling a swimming pool. *Could it be the Hidden Waters?* Frank wondered. Maples, red leaves fluttering and occasionally falling, were spaced evenly around the lawn. One lone swimmer was doing laps in the heated pool.

Frank laid his notepad and pencil on the black lacquered desk. A vase of fresh yellow chrysanthemums adorned one corner. He helped Solnitz maneuver into a tan leather armchair alongside the desk, then draped his jacket over the high-backed, black leather desk chair. Loosening his tie, he opened the top button of his shirt and sat down, poised to take notes.

Solnitz looked at Frank. "You're the first."

"The first, Mr. Solnitz?"

"The first reporter. And it's Doctor Solnitz, but you can call me Albert."

If Wilma had mentioned that Albert was a doctor, Frank had missed it in his somnolence two hours earlier. *Weary Warrior*'s dust jacket didn't mention it either. "Really? What kind of doctor?"

"Medical. I've been retired for twenty-seven years." He looked absently out the window. "I'm surprised more reporters haven't come. By now they should be clamoring for interviews."

"It's still early," Frank replied, deciding not to mention what he had heard on the radio. "As a matter of fact, I didn't hear through the usual channels. Wilma Rachlik, the night nurse, called me first thing this morning. She knew I'd be interested."

"Really? That battle-axe?" He stroked his chin. "Which paper did you say you were with?"

"Uh—I write for *The Daily Chronicle*."

"Used to be a good paper, but I don't read it anymore. Too opinionated." Solnitz leaned toward Frank. "Have you read my novels? I've written eight, you know, and a volume of short stories and one of essays."

"Some of them." Before Solnitz could embarrass him by asking which ones or how many, Frank went on. "Isn't there one, *Weary Warrior*, set in the 1950s in which the leading character—a writer, I forget his name—leaves the United States for Europe just when he was getting recognized? I wasn't sure why he left." What Frank meant was that the dust jacket never explained it.

Albert leaned forward excitedly. "My first

novel! That character would be Angus Schwartz. I modeled him after a friend of mine who got recognized when he worked for the WPA during the Great Depression. You probably weren't born then. In World War Two, I had Angus fight in the Pacific, get wounded, and receive a Silver Star and Purple Heart. After the War, the reactionaries, as we used to call them, branded the New Deal a plot to have the Communists take over. Schwartz wasn't a Communist but they blacklisted him."

"You mean he couldn't get his work published?"

Solnitz nodded. "I gave him three choices in the novel: He could name names; he could become a shoe salesman; or he could go to France, where the people and the government were more tolerant." He looked straight at Frank. "What would you have done with such a character?"

"Well, becoming a shoe salesman wouldn't have been very glamorous. And I suppose you wouldn't be happy making him a stool pigeon."

"Yes, I really had no choice."

Frank continued. "How old were you when you wrote *Weary Warrior*?"

"Seventy-three; eight years after I retired from medicine. It was a finalist for the National Book Award, you know."

"I know," Frank acknowledged. Changing the subject, he asked, "Why did you start writing so late?"

Solnitz thought for a moment. "I've been late doing many things. My wife almost left me because I was always late. I was also late talking, not until age three, but when I started I spoke in complete sentences, or so my parents told me."

"I suppose you had nothing to say before that," Frank joked.

"It's possible," he shrugged, "and sometimes afterwards, too. In high school, an English teacher, Mr. Mantinband, gave us an assignment to foreshadow an event in a story. Foreshadowing would have been easy if I could have thought up an event. I almost flunked the course. I've written all my novels since I retired as a doctor."

"Your medical practice must have given you lots of plots. Many M.D.s have become writers."

Solnitz thought for a moment. "Let's see—" He started to count on his fingers. "Chekhov, Somerset Maugham, Conan Doyle, William Carlos Williams. I'm probably leaving some out. For the thousands of doctors in the world, that's precious few. Oh, a few others—Robin Cook, Michael Crichton, for example—wrote pot boilers, not serious fiction." A smile crossed his face. "You know what Chekhov said about being a doctor and a writer?" Frank shook his head. Solnitz gazed at Renoir's *The Bather*, trying to bring the quote into focus: "Medicine is my lawful wife, and literature is my mistress. When I get fed up with one, I spend the night with the other."

They both chuckled. Solnitz continued. "Seriously though, you know why most doctors don't write fiction?" He did not wait for Frank to answer. "In medicine as in science, it's a crime to fabricate. You theorize about what's wrong with your patient, but then you have to collect evidence. In writing fiction, you can make up the evidence. It took five years after I quit medicine before I was able to fabricate, to make up stories, to make characters do what I wanted in order to make a point."

Solnitz looked out the window; Frank followed his glance. The swimmer was climbing the ladder at the near end of the pool. She removed a bathing cap and shook her white hair until it spread down to her shoulders. "That's the widow Lewison. Not a bad figure for seventy, wouldn't you say?"

"Yes, she's trim all right," Frank agreed.

"She goes to all that trouble—swimming, treadmill, even weights—just to keep fit. She hasn't given me or any other man here a tumble."

"Aren't you a little old for her?"

"I know much bigger age spreads, don't you? We'll see what happens when I bring home the prize money." Solnitz stopped, still looking at Mrs. Lewison. Then he continued *sotto voce*. "To tell you the truth, I like to look at the fair sex; fucking is no longer an option. A kiss, a little pat here and there, that's my pleasure." He looked at Frank. "Please don't say that in your story."

Both men gazed at Mrs. Lewison as she wrapped a robe around her shoulders and walked back to the building.

Frank turned the conversation to the Nobel Prize. "Were you surprised when you got the, uh—call?"

"Not entirely. I knew that very prominent authors, including some Laureates, had nominated me. In all modesty, I thought it was long overdue." Frank was about to ask for the names of those who had nominated Solnitz—he could fact-check afterwards—but Albert went right on. "You know, I am the oldest person ever to be awarded the Nobel Prize in Literature."

"Really?"

"Yes, I keep track of things. Theodor Mommsen won it in 1902 at age 85. Now I am the oldest."

"Wilma Rachlik says you haven't written anything since you've been here."

"How would she know?" Albert asked angrily. Is she the Gestapo, looking inside my computer? My agent died a few years ago; he was eighty-two, a youngster. Nobody takes an old man seriously, so my work lies hidden on my hard drive. I've been working on a tragi-comedy, *Growing Old Is Not for Sissies*. Now with the prize, I won't have trouble getting an agent. I bet it will be published next year."

"How did you react when they called you from Stockholm?"

Solnitz leaned back and closed his eyes. "I wasn't expecting anyone to call at that hour. At first, I didn't understand the man's accent. I said, 'You must have the wrong number!' I started to hang up, but I heard him pronounce my name. Then he told me I had won the Nobel Prize in Literature."

"What did you say?"

"It's about time!"

Frank asked, "'It's about time?' Do you think that was wise?"

"Wise or not, if they waited much longer I'd be dead. I'm ninety-two, you know."

"What did he say next?"

"He seemed to be shouting something in another language I didn't understand."

"Then what happened?"

"I was so excited I dropped the phone and ran out to the nurses' station to tell, uh, your friend Rachlik. She didn't believe me." Solnitz looked wistfully at Renoir's *Bather* again.

"Rachlik told me you were in your underwear, shouting, 'I won, I won.'"

"If the call had come two minutes later, I would have been stark naked. Here's what happened: I had just taken my shirt and pants off and was brushing my teeth. While I brushed, the phone rang. I rinsed my mouth and got to it as fast as I could; on the fourth ring, I think. Besides, what else was I going to put on? I'll have to rent a tuxedo for Stockholm, you know."

"What did Rachlik say when you ran out shouting?"

"She didn't say anything. She got an aide—as if she needed help—to get me back to my apartment. I kept saying, 'You don't understand, you don't understand.' Finally, they sat me down on the sofa. The old bitch asked, 'What don't we understand, Albert?' I said, 'I've been trying to tell you, they called to tell me I won. At that point my phone started to beep rapidly. As Rachlik picked it up, I could hear the operator say, 'If you'd like to make a call, please hang up and dial again.' Rachlik hung up the phone. 'Too bad you don't have Caller ID, Albert, then we could tell where the call came from.' She seemed to calm down a bit, came back to the sofa, threw a robe over my shoulders, and sat down next to me. 'Anyway, Albert, who called you?' she asked. 'What did you win?' 'The Committee to tell me I won the Nobel Prize,' I told her. 'They give lots of Nobel Prizes, Albert,' the bitch said, 'Did you win them all?' 'No, just the one for literature,' I replied. When she asked me what I'd written I went to the bookcase, pulled out three of my books, and tossed them to her, one at a time. She didn't even bother to look at them."

"Nurse Rachlik said you were violent."

"Violent?" He raised his voice for the first time. "Does she have proof? Does she have any bruises? The only thing that got bruised were my books; the spine on one split." Solnitz stopped to admire the chrysanthemums in the vase. "I'll tell you what I think: Your friend Nurse Rachlik doesn't believe a ninety-two-year-old, or a seventy-year-old for that matter, could write coherently, or be published, let alone win the Nobel Prize in Literature." He bent forward and pulled a soiled handkerchief from his back pocket and wiped saliva from his lips. He looked at the courtyard, now empty, then back at Frank. "Maybe you don't believe me either."

A knock on the door interrupted them. Simultaneously the two men said, "Come in."

Dolores entered. "Sorry to interrupt." She smiled at Frank as she turned to Solnitz. "Time for your medicine, Albert." She was wearing a loose smock over a snug, light blue blouse with the top two buttons undone, and tight-fitting black slacks. (*Hidden Waters* discouraged uniforms.) Bending forward, she handed Solnitz two identical pills and a glass of water.

"Why two?" Solnitz asked, peering at her cleavage.

"You were very excited last night, Albert. The doctor said to double your dose of Olanzapine, at least for a little while."

"These pills will kill me before they'll tamp down my, my"—he was groping for the right word—"enthusiasm."

"Don't be silly, Albert," she slapped his arm playfully. "We wouldn't give you anything harmful."

He swallowed the pills and handed the cup

back. As she turned to leave, Solnitz gripped the left arm of his chair and raised himself up. Extending his right arm, he called out "Dolores, dear" as he tried to pat her bottom. She turned around, glancing at his outstretched arm. "Maybe my guest would like a glass of water and you could refill mine." She returned a minute later with a pitcher of ice water and another glass. This time she did not bend as she picked up Albert's glass. She bent to fill Frank's.

"Thank you," Frank said. "We're almost finished." Dolores left. Taking a sip of water, Frank asked Albert, "Do you like it here?"

Solnitz looked after Dolores. "Not bad cleavage." He turned to Frank. "I'm sorry, what did you say?" Frank repeated his question. "What's not to like? A good-looking nurse like Dolores, a studio apartment, lovely grounds, my own television, stereo, and, of course, my computer. I couldn't survive without my computer."

"How long have you been here?"

"Five years. After my wife died, I decided to try this place. In the old days, when your children didn't want you—or you didn't want them—it would be the nursing home. Now we have these assisted living facilities. As I say, 'What's not to like'? Of course, it's expensive, and my royalties are slowing down. Now that I'll have a million dollars, I might buy my own place and hire some nice young ladies to take care of me. Maybe Mrs. Lewison will be interested."

"A million dollars?"

"The prize money. It's still a million, isn't it?" Frank didn't answer. "Of course, that doesn't buy as much these days, but still, I wouldn't complain."

Frank stood up. "Well, Albert, you've given me

plenty to write about. I'm so glad I had the opportunity to be the first to talk with you."

Solnitz lifted himself with the help of his walker. He stuck out his right hand, warmer and drier than when they first met. Putting his left hand over Frank's, Solnitz beamed. "I enjoyed our conversation almost as much as winning the prize. Tell me your name again."

"Sigman. Frank Sigman." Frank trailed Albert back toward the lobby where he bid him goodbye.
*

After Frank left, Albert pushed his walker down the corridor to the activities room. He banged the door open with his walker, interrupting the social organizer who had just shouted "N 37" to twenty-four other residents clustered six to a table looking down at their cards. Instead of taking a seat, Solnitz shuffled to the front of the group. "Excuse me," he said. "I have an announcement." A few people raised their heads. "I got a call from Stockholm last night. I've won the Nobel Prize in Literature."

A few more looked up. One, still looking down, shouted "Bingo!" and everyone applauded.

At seven that evening, Frank Sigman received a call from Wilma. "Well, Frank, what do you think?"

"About Dr. Solnitz?"

Several times after the interview, Frank had started to phone the editor at *The Daily Chronicle* with a scoop. Sometimes he stopped because he felt he'd be doing something immoral, like insider trading. Other times he doubted that Solnitz had won the prize. He'd had other patients, especially when he was training at University Hospital, who convinced him of their fantastic tales. Rachlik was never taken in, he had to admit. But maybe this case was different.

"Did Dr. Solnitz have any more outbursts?" he asked Wilma.

"Not exactly. He's got the other residents congratulating him. They want to have a party in his honor. You were right; he was a writer, his books are in our library." For the first time he heard doubt creep into her voice. "You don't think he actually—"

He cut her off. "Why don't we listen to the news tomorrow morning. I think his mind is sound enough for him to stay at Hidden Waters, Wilma," he paused, "except maybe to go to Stockholm."

*

In his diary entry for that October day in 1999, Sigman wrote that it was plausible that Solnitz had received a call the previous night from the Academy. "When he insulted the caller by saying 'It's about time,'" Sigman wrote, "the Nobel representative might have bickered with Solnitz in Swedish. Overcome with excitement, Solnitz could have dropped the phone and run into the hall to announce his victory. The caller could have hung up in consternation by the time Solnitz returned to the room with Wilma Rachlik, and then postponed announcement of the award until he could consult with his colleagues." Sigman concluded his entry that night, "I've set my alarm to be awake for the eight o'clock news tomorrow morning."

Sigman's diary had no further entries regarding Albert Solnitz. Two days later, his only entry was: "Gunter Grass of Germany won the Nobel Prize in Literature today."

Acknowledgments

In the Preface, I wrote that most of the stories in this volume were "drawn from experience—my own and others I've known." I gratefully acknowledge those "others," but it would betray an implicit trust, and in some cases friendship, if I revealed their names. I did not seek their permission before fictionalizing them. Some of them might not even recognize themselves in the characters and/or plot. In two cases in which I was sure they would, I told them confidentially what I'd done. It cost me the friendship of one.

Several of these stories were vetted in the Desert Writers Workshop in Las Cruces New Mexico over ten years ago. I credit this group, and Prof. Kevin McIlvoy, its leader for most of the time, with starting my authorial career by encouraging me to write while at the same teaching me the value of constructive criticism. Since then, I have found sharing my work-in-progress with others, either one-on-one, workshops, or writing groups, in person or online, to be a rewarding path to improvement. I've started a few of these and I want to thank the three stalwarts of the Writers Workshop at Little House, Menlo Park CA, Glenna Houle, Peter Mork, and Linda Schneider for their help with the stories I was working on in 2017 to 19. More recently, Johanna Sessford, Elaine and Tom Schneider (no relation to Linda) allowed me to read the stories aloud to them and offered cogent criticism. One story in particular underwent a barrage of criticism. I especially want to thank Amy Catania, my muse for *The Bethune Murals*, for setting me on the right path.

Before publishing my first novel when I was seventy-seven, I used the *Guide to Literary Agents* to identify agents who might be interested enough in my work to help me find a publisher. After a few futile months I concluded that I might be dead before I found one. Consequently, I formed Cloudsplitter Press (www.cloudsplitterpress.com)—Eva Cohen, to whom these stories are dedicated, set up the website for me—and decided to self-publish *Axton Landing* and all my subsequent novels. Eva designed the elegant covers. For the last two novels, I was fortunate to engage Lynn Stegner as my editor. I was a student of hers in an Advanced Novel Workshop at Stanford's Continuing Education Program. Lynn did the same excellent job with these stories, continuing my education as a writer. She patiently taught me that I was much more constrained in writing a short story than a novel. You the reader must be the judge of how well I have succeeded.

www.ingramcontent.com/pod-product-compliance
Lightning Source LLC
Chambersburg PA
CBHW030505260626
47157CB00005B/1667